the
Other Side
of Summer

the Other Side of Summer

EMILY GALE

HARPER
An Imprint of HarperCollinsPublishers

HarperCollins
PUBLISHERS
Since 1817

Library of Congress Control Number: 2016961850
ISBN 978-0-06-265674-2 (trade bdg.)

17 18 19 20 21 PC/LSCH 10 9 8 7 6 5 4 3 2 1
❖
First American Edition
Originally published by Random House Australia in 2016

For my small but mighty girls:
my daughter, Madeleine, and my sister, Eleanor

"Hope" is the thing with feathers—
That perches in the soul—
And sings the tune without the words—
And never stops—at all—
Emily Dickinson

And above all, watch with glittering eyes
the whole world around you because
the greatest secrets are always hidden
in the most unlikely places.
Those who don't believe in magic will never find it.
Roald Dahl

part one

ENGLAND

the other side of
the Story

The doorbell pierced the grim quiet of our house. Nobody moved. I knew this even though I couldn't see the others. Our house stirred and breathed with us like old places do. I imagined us four freezing in our separate roosting spots. We, the Jackmans, were never called on unexpectedly anymore.

The doorbell rang again. This time I heard the house fidget. As I poked my head around the doorway of the living room I saw the others coming out of their hiding places. Dad and Wren downstairs like me, and Mum on the upstairs landing, peering over the railing. I told myself it would be the postman at the door, or someone selling dishcloths.

It was the police.

"Mr. Jackman?"

"Yes?"

"I'm Detective Constable Patel and this is Police Constable Brooks. Sorry to disturb you on a Saturday." She spoke gently and with concerned eyes, which we were used to.

By now, my sister was beside me. The police officers gave her a look. Most people did.

They'd come to return our lost property: an Ibanez Artwood. It was a dark brown guitar with a burst of orange around the bridge that bled outward like a fierce sunset. We'd thought it was lost forever. It was supposed to have been blown to pieces, turned to ashes. But there it was. Whole.

"It's been assessed and cataloged," said one of the officers.

I wasn't paying attention to whichever one of them was speaking. My eyes were on the Ibanez Artwood, returned to us from the dead.

———

After they'd gone, Dad laid the guitar in the solid case that had been sitting empty for weeks.

"It's perfect," he said, with a knot in his voice. "Not a single mark on it."

How? I thought. I remembered all the times Mum had shouted at Floyd not to take his guitar busking without a case. This was usually when he was already halfway out the door. He'd smile and say, "Don't worry, Mum. I'll be careful with it."

Having the guitar back was like returning to the day when we'd lost my brother. I don't think Floyd and his Ibanez Artwood had ever been separated before. Now we had one without the other.

The rest of my family scattered to deal with a new wave of pain. Dad went to the kitchen table with his laptop. All I could see was his face poking over the top, as unreadable as an old gravestone. Wren claimed our bedroom—which made it out of bounds to me. Mum shut the door on hers and the low moaning sounds she made scared me more than anything.

So I stayed in the living room with the Ibanez Artwood.

The guitar case had a purple velvet lining. Somewhere there was a photo of me curled up inside it like a caterpillar in a cocoon, grinning at my brother, who had been behind the camera. I felt a shiver and closed the lid.

———————

That night I couldn't sleep. I crept downstairs when the house was free of Jackman noises, when the only

5

sounds were the old pipes and the fridge. Kneeling by the case, I flicked the catches open, then stopped.

What did I hope for? A message? A sign?

I could remember two things about my sixth birthday party. The first was the cake: a bright red, lopsided toadstool with tiny fairy figurines dancing underneath it. The second was watching Floyd make our cat disappear in a magic box. He'd lowered her into it, closed the lid, spun the box around, and hey-presto! No Charlotte. Even after I knew about the mirror and the secret compartment, I still thought my big brother was capable of things that ordinary humans weren't.

I opened the lid of the case and felt almost surprised to find the Ibanez Artwood still inside.

I lifted it out, careful not to touch the strings. To hold it was one thing but to hear it would break me apart.

Its curved body was a tight fit between my lap and my chin. Floyd had been teaching me to play on his spare guitar since I was ten. That one was a little smaller and had always lived on a hook in Floyd's bedroom. His door was permanently shut now. In my imagination, opening it would release our horrible screams of that first day. Music had been the last thing on our minds since Floyd had gone. But here it was again in the shape of the Ibanez Artwood. I couldn't help following the guitar's trail back to Waterloo Station.

The bomb had been inside the big clock, hidden in the space between the four faces. We didn't know what Floyd had been doing there that day. Maybe that made it worse for us, but it was hard to tell when it was already this painful. Too often I thought about the moment the bomb exploded.

When I pictured it, I slowed down the ticks and tocks of the clock so I could try to understand. Tick . . . tock. A tick became a tock. A tick became a tock became a tick became a tock, until a tick became a deafening thunder of noise, the ear-splitting roar of a monster released from a tiny box.

Tick-tock. Tick-tock. Tick-BOOM.

And no tock.

I imagined time had held its breath then, as I was doing now. I pictured mixed-up matter flying in all directions. Yet random objects had survived, completely whole. For example, the Ibanez Artwood. Who could explain to me how that could be, when bones had splintered violently into dust? Tick, you're alive. Tock, you're dead.

My brother, gone.

I rested my cheek on the guitar. It was a survivor. The guitar that never left Floyd's side was somehow in the right place at the right time, even though it had been in the hands of my brother, who was in the wrong place at the wrong time.

The Ibanez Artwood had to be back for a reason. It was so familiar but now it was also strange, like lost things are once they're found, because it had been somewhere I hadn't. Somehow I knew its return was the sign of a different, unexpected ending. Suddenly it felt like more than an object, more than mahogany and steel, almost warm-blooded.

In that moment I decided it was my brother's epilogue, and I wasn't going to let it out of my sight.

the other side of
a friend

The low sun was behind us as we walked home from school. For weeks London had been in its winter uniform of bare trees and drizzle, but today the sky had taken my breath away with its ultra-blue. I could almost taste the color in the icy air on my tongue. Now and then I looked around to catch the last of the daylight waving its arms through the tight gaps between houses. Our shadows spilled out of our feet on the uneven pavement, trying to get home before us. Unlike my shadow, I was in no hurry.

Mal's shadow was so tall next to mine that we looked more like a mum and a little girl than two best friends. But that's what we were.

"Watch out for the dog poo!" said Mal, pointing to a spot on my side of the pavement just ahead.

Like I said, best friends.

The definition of a good day had changed since Floyd had gone, but I'd had one today. This afternoon had been so busy that I'd only thought about him a few times and I'd even smiled when I walked past the special framed photo of him in the corridor outside the principal's office. Only Mal had noticed, and because she was my best friend she'd smiled too, and didn't say anything. That was a big thing for Mal because she was a real talker.

Right now she was raving about a new manga she was reading. It was set in the future and sounded complicated. When I used to read, I'd choose stories set in the past. They seemed safer to me. Mal was the adventurous one.

Even though I'd completely lost the thread of what she was saying, half-listening to Mal was like an ice pack on a throbbing bruise. But nothing much got past her.

"Hey, what are you thinking about?"

I watched her shadow-elbow come toward my shadow-arm, but it was still a surprise to feel her touch. I smiled at her. "Sorry, I'm in a daze as usual." I didn't mean to shut her out.

"You know you can tell me anything," she said.

"I know. I do tell you things." Which was true. I just didn't tell her everything anymore. "I was thinking that I wish my house would jump up and put itself in a faraway spot so we could keep walking home forever."

"Let's walk the long way then."

So we did, but even the long way ran out too soon. At my front gate, we both looked at the door and then at each other.

"I could come in," said Mal.

I looked up and saw the curtains drawn over Mum's bedroom window. "Another time, okay?"

It was awkward then, because I could tell that Mal wanted to give me a hug. I hadn't felt like hugging anyone for a long time. I didn't want to hurt her feelings but this was one of the ways I stayed strong, by keeping people away. I was on a different island now. Most girls at school pretended not to see me, anyway. Losing a brother is ugly. As ugly to them as losing an eye.

But it must have been hard for Mal to understand. She had never looked away from me. That smile and the gap between her two front teeth—which she said she'd never get braces for because then she'd just look like everyone else—was my daily reminder of what happiness was. Just one hug couldn't hurt, could it?

Suddenly the front door opened and Dad appeared. "There you are!" he said. Dad hated for me to be late home.

I'll admit I was relieved that he'd interrupted the moment.

"How was your day?" Dad seemed to be overacting, as if he was still in work mode. He had a goofy smile and was still dressed in his dark blue suit with the plastic badge that said "Doug Jackman, Real Estate Agent."

"Good," I said. The word was as small and hard as a peanut.

"Hi, Mr. Jackman," said Mal. She waved with her fingers while her thumbs were looped under the straps of her backpack, which looked funny—a bit like she was a tall bird with tiny hatchling wings.

"Hi there, Malinda. I'd invite you in but I've got something important to tell Summer."

"You have?" My heart started drumming the way it always did now when anyone said they had something to tell me. "I'd better go in. Bye, Mal."

"See you tomorrow." Mal walked backward for a little way, as if she was as worried as I was about what Dad's "something important" could be. Then she smiled, and winked, and turned around to walk the short distance home.

"Take your coat off. Put your bag down," said Dad,

while I was in the middle of doing exactly both of those things. He seemed nervous, but the excited kind.

"Is this something bad?" I said.

"Not at all! Something good, I hope."

He scraped his hair back with his hand, and his hairline, which already had two deep inlets on either side, seemed to recede even further. His suit was getting tighter. Mum was the opposite; she was shrinking.

I followed Dad into the front room. Everything looked normal, except for Dad, who had started bouncing on his toes.

"Summer. I've come up with a plan."

the other side of
the plan

I couldn't wait to hear about the plan because our family desperately needed one. Things were bad. We were a wreckage. I thought Dad meant something like therapy, or even just a nice day out.

He said it to me like a magic word, an abracadabra painted with his right hand in the space above my head. "Austraaaaliaaa!"

For a second the ground dropped from my feet as if the bit of floor I was standing on was a portal and I was going to fall straight through to that faraway place. But I found something to cling onto. "Oh, you mean for a holiday."

Dad had shifty eyes. "Not exactly." And a sheepish

grin. "Well, not at all. Think about it, Summer. Australia!"
He looked at the word still dangling over my head like
a colorful piñata in our house of gloom.

I shook my head. I tried to say the word back, to
return it to Dad like an unwanted gift.

"Australia?" The syllables were fat and awkward in
my mouth. "No way, Dad. We can't."

But he looked so sure, and so happy about it.

"When?" I added.

"Two weeks!" Dad whacked his dumb piñata
and watched the idea rain down hard onto my head,
causing tiny hairline fractures in my skull. Two weeks?
This couldn't be real.

I thought of Floyd then. The memory of him always
showed up unexpectedly when I was halfway through
a conversation, or during loud applause at a school
assembly, or when I was waiting quietly for the kettle to
boil. And my heart would go *boom, boom, boom* trying
to expand into the space he'd left. It would swell and
stutter out of my control.

I knew this feeling would pass. It did every time,
which was a relief that also made me feel rotten and
guilty. *My* heart was still beating.

Questions about Dad's plan started to roll out of
me. "But how? Why? What about our life here? What
about my friends? What about Gran? And for how

long? And . . ." I came full circle back to "*How?*" As in, "How can you think this will help us, Dad?"

He counted his answers on his fingers. "How? On a plane, of course, sweetheart. Why? Because we need to get away from London, and Australia used to be my home, chicken. What about our life here? I think you know the answer to that. You'll make *new* friends. You were saying the other day that Malinda is the only one you really like." His eyes crinkled in sympathy.

My jaw clenched, telling me I should have kept my mouth shut.

"And Gran will visit, my little dot."

Sweetheart, chicken, and little dot: they weren't exactly superhero names, so how was I going to prevent this disaster on my own?

There was one question he hadn't answered, and all I had to do was cross my arms and stare at him.

"How long?" he said. He bent down so our faces were level and threw the word toward me gently, the way you throw a ball to a little kid who can't catch. "Forever."

He meant it.

The room became an airless pocket. I *hated* him for doing this to me, and reached for the nearest thing that could hurt him:

"What does *Mum* think?"

There was a telltale pause, and he straightened up. "She's excited." He swallowed. Dad was a terrible liar. I knew for certain that Mum would not be excited about this plan. Excitement was one lost thing in our house, and Mum was another.

"What about Wren? She won't go without a fight." My sister could breathe fire about Dad's choice of breakfast cereal, let alone something like this.

"You make it sound as if I'm hauling you off to prison."

"That's what it used to be!"

"Now you're just being silly," he snapped. For the first time since I'd walked through the door, I felt wary of him. Perhaps he saw the look on my face because he touched my chin and smiled. "You don't know anything about the place."

And I didn't want to. It was hard enough getting through the days here. How would we cope in a strange country?

Now Dad was giving me a look that said it was him and me against the world—or at least against Mum and Wren, the lost causes. . . .

No, no, no. I would never join him on this. "It can't happen, Dad."

"*Australia*, Summer." As if I had forgotten what we were talking about! "It's an amazing place, just you wait and see."

"You're crazy."

"No, I'm right about this."

"We can't."

"Of course we can."

"But I love it here."

"You'll love it *there*."

"It doesn't make any sense. *DAD, IT DOESN'T MAKE ANY SENSE!*" It was like shouting through thick glass.

"You have to trust me. Don't cry, sweetheart."

"I can't help it." Feelings I couldn't even name had taken me over like ants on a crumb. "I can't believe . . ." My voice thinned out and I ran out of words. I was half-blind with tears. Dad reached out to touch my arm and I pulled away as hard as I could.

Somehow I'd failed a test that I hadn't been expecting. And now I just wanted this moment to be over. To reverse out of this room, back to the front gate with Mal ten minutes ago. I'd hug her and never let go.

Every tick of the mantelpiece clock sounded like scorn. Until suddenly Dad's arms were around me and I was sobbing loudly into his jacket. A new moment had already gobbled up the last one. Half of me wanted to be near him and the other half felt trapped. I hated him. Even as he squashed me like a bear in the way I used to like. Even when he whispered into the top of my head that I was his precious girl.

Hated him. Hated Mum. Hated Wren. Hated Floyd for dying. Hated me. Felt sick for hating. My heart was worn out.

Finally I stopped crying, and when I did I told myself Dad's plan would go away like an imaginary friend if I just let him believe it was real, for now.

"Well?" he said.

"Well . . ." My nose was stuffed; my eyes felt like I'd been punched. "It would be cool to see a kangaroo."

Pretend words. We weren't going anywhere. Mum would stop it. Wren would. Gran would. *Someone* would. Kangaroos, sunshine, the other side of the planet: that wasn't for us.

Dad stroked my hair and told me about flights and rental houses and schools like it was a bedtime story, but his words were skimming stones. I didn't believe in his stories the way I used to. What I believed in now was a giant, bird-shaped shadow that soared over people and swooped down at random to pick them off. I believed that the pain of missing someone could twist you, shrink you, cut you to pieces, take all your color away.

I needed to be with the one person who'd seen all that change in me and was still hanging around.

Someone who could tell me that this plan wouldn't happen.

"I'm going to Mal's house."

"Of course," said Dad. "Whatever you need to do." I let him wipe a leftover tear from my cheek with his thumb.

the other side of despair

Dad walked me to Mal's even though I'd been walking there on my own since I was nine because Mum had always wanted us to be free-range kids. It was only around the corner but I felt as weak and sore as if I'd been in an accident, so it didn't hurt to let him.

Mal answered the door and looked surprised and happy to see me, until she saw the look on my face. Dad said he'd come back for me in a couple of hours.

"What's happened?" she said as soon as she closed the door.

"Where's your mum?"

"On the computer."

"Where's your dad?"

"On the other computer. What's going on, Summer? You're freaking me out."

"I'll tell you everything. Just give me a second. I think I'm in shock."

In Mal's tiny hallway I breathed in and out deeply and tried to imagine how I would tell her. Two pairs of giant shoes (Mal's and her dad's) were lined up next to one pair of tiny ones (Mal's mum's). I slipped mine off and put them alongside. It was a shoes-off house, but as Mal's mum, Deeta, had explained to me a long time ago, this wasn't because she was worried about her carpet getting dirty—it was because she wanted her guests' feet to sink into it and feel at home. I'd always felt that way here.

"Let's go to my room," said Mal. "Via the kitchen." She knew me so well. Before, Mum had been in charge of what we ate at home and there was always something delicious. Now it was Dad's job and his basic rule was no junk food or anything nice, ever. I knew why; it was obvious: he wanted to keep us safe from every danger he could predict because he hadn't been able to save Floyd from an unpredictable one. So I didn't argue. Mostly he cooked unpronounceable things that tasted like the ground. How he was actually getting fatter on this stuff was an unexplained mystery.

So these days I got my fix of junk at Mal's. She led

the way upstairs with a box of Dunkin' Donuts.

Mal's bedroom was how I imagined the inside of a gypsy caravan would look. Candles burning, draped sequinned material, dreamcatchers, crystal figurines, silk cushions with frayed edges from Camden Market. The colors were like a box of crayons: burnt orange, brick red, electric lime, and Pacific blue.

But as soon as we walked in I felt a wave of nausea. Something in there had poked a sleeping ghoul in my belly. . . . Incense. It was my memory of that particular smell. Mal had collected so many flavors that almost every time I went into her room it smelled different, but this was sandalwood and it took me straight back to that day. . . .

We'd had a sleepover. It was nearly lunchtime but we were still in our pajamas. Deeta had come into the room without knocking, fighting her breathlessness and trying to say calmly that I was needed home straightaway.

I was seeing it all now, close-up and distorted through a fish-eye lens. Deeta's eyes wide and scared. Deeta's hand reaching out to take mine. Deeta's echoing voice saying, "I have to take you home. I can't tell you why, Summer—your mum and dad will," and Mal and I both begging her to. "Just tell us!" Mal was shouting. "Can't you see how upset she is?" The tumble of our footsteps down the staircase . . .

There the scene zoomed in so tight that the only picture I had was of my feet in flip-flops taking me home. Left foot, right foot, left foot, right foot, neon-yellow toenails we'd painted the night before, walking toward something so horrible that already those feet didn't seem like they could be mine.

"Summer, what's wrong?" said Mal, here and now, in her bedroom.

I looked at my friend and I knew she didn't deserve any of the awful things I'd been thinking since that day. (Why did you make me come for a sleepover the night before my brother died, so I missed his last moments? Why do you have to burn that stupid incense? Why are you looking at me so kindly when I'm like this? Don't you know that I never took that neon-yellow nail polish off, and that even now there are traces of it?) I knew all of it was unfair, but that didn't make it go away.

"I'm fine. Sorry. You honestly won't believe my dad."

We sat opposite each other on a sheepskin rug. The Dunkin' Donuts box was between us like a ouija board.

"Ready? Okay. Dad wants us to go and live in Australia."

She stared at me as if I hadn't spoken. I counted the seconds until the exact moment the words hit her. One, two, three, f—

24

"He what? That's not even funny, Summer."

There was fire in her expression, so I fanned the flames. "No joke. In two weeks. He's booked the flights. He's even found us a school."

"Wait, wait, hang on a second. Australia? To live? But . . . Australia?"

"Exactly."

"This *cannot* happen. We can't let it, Summer!"

"I know." I took a donut. "We totally can't."

Now that I'd said it out loud I felt myself relax a bit. It was nice to agree with Mal. It made it feel almost as if the plan had nothing to do with me. Let her take over. Let me live on bright and brilliant Planet Mal.

"This is definitely, definitely, *definitely* not happening, Summer. Definitely." Every scrap of horror and disbelief that I'd been feeling appeared like magic in my best friend's face. "I'm outraged," she said, undoing the difficult job of crossing her legs so she could stand again. "I need to pace."

Mal listed all the reasons Dad's plan was horrible. Some of them were excellently argued, such as "Changing high school midyear could have a negative effect on your grades, Summer Jackman." She was full-naming me now and her voice sounded exactly like her mum's. Deeta spoke perfect English with an Indian accent that made all the words sound more

dramatic—she rolled her *r*'s and cushioned her *t*'s—
and I loved to listen to her almost as much as I loved
to listen to Mal. Deeta was bossy and confident and
kind, too, just like Mal. Stu, Mal's dad, was six feet five,
Scottish, quiet and freckly, and you didn't hear from
him very much. He wrote poetry.

"Summer Jackman, listen to me," said Mal. "We have
to stop this. You cannot live in that hot place. Look at
you, you're like a beautiful . . . snowflake."

I nodded and chewed.

"All we need is a plan of our own, Summer. Just
let me figure it out. Plan A, coming up." She lit more
candles, changed the incense to jasmine, and put on a
new album she'd downloaded called *Positive Energy*.

I took yet another donut. In that moment I felt like
if I stayed put on the soft rug eating junk and listening to Mal, my head spinning in a sugar rush, Australia
would stay far away from my reality. She could fix this.

Mal had been my best friend since we were four. It
was easy to explain why I loved her: she was open to
everything, no matter how impossible it seemed. Some
people at school thought that made her gullible, or
even crazy—not that they'd ever dare say that to her
face because, without being the most popular girl, Mal
was the kind of confident that made people suspicious,
as if she had a secret they didn't know about. Her kind

of open was strong, and she was fearless about it. If Mal had to paint a picture it would be enormous and bright. If she had to sing a song it would be loud and joyful. It would also be completely out of tune, but that didn't matter to Mal.

Then there was what she believed in. She'd almost made up her own religion. My best friend believed in everything. Really! Everything. She salvaged bits from here and there like a magpie. In her bedroom she had buddhas, a poster of three Hindu goddesses, and a sculpture of the Greek goddess Athena that she'd made in art class. She even believed that aliens and UFOs and ghostly spirits could be out there. Sometimes the details of what she was saying got tangled, but when I was with her she made sense to me. And that was why I'd been trying so hard to ignore the gap that had opened up between us since Floyd had died. I wanted to close it up again, not make it bigger.

Right now I needed to believe in life working out for the best, the way Mal did. She had her hopes pinned on anything and everything. If something seemed impossible, unlikely, or just too good to be true, you could bet Mal would pin a hope on it.

But what I'd realized (but would never, ever tell her) was this: she wasn't picky enough. She was pinning tiny hopes in so many places that no big miracles could happen. Maybe miracle power was leaking out slowly from all the holes her pins had made.

I only had a single hope, one single pin: to stay here, where we belonged. All our memories of Floyd lived here. And the only thing worse than painful memories would be none at all.

———————

By the time Dad came to collect me, there wasn't just a Plan A: Mal's plans went right up to E. I felt a tiny bit dubious about all of them for different reasons but I didn't say anything. Anyway, if I knew Mal, she'd have a brilliant Plan F that she hadn't told me about tucked up her sleeve.

I walked out of the Gupta-McIntosh house where the air was 78 percent nitrogen, 21 percent oxygen, 1 percent argon and, more important, millions of pretty molecules of optimism floating about in between.

Mal jumped down from the doorstep and before I knew what was happening she was hugging me. "I'll text you," she whispered.

Dad and I were only halfway down the street when it arrived.

Spoiler: everything is going to turn out OK. Love, M

the other side of
Mum

We had dinner in front of the TV that night. The menu was nothing to get excited about—brown pasta and salad sprinkled with seeds that kept getting caught in my teeth. I could feel my stomach grinding the food as if I had gizzard stones in there. I kept glancing round at the hallway phone, just visible through the living room doorway, waiting for Plan A to kick in.

Mum was downstairs with us, which was what everyone wanted even though it made sitting on the sofa feel more like perching on a cliff edge. It was still better than sensing her on the other side of the ceiling. Up there she was a whispery ghost, and the dark weight of her not wanting to be near us pressed through.

"If everyone's finished, I've got something to show you," said Dad. He switched off the TV.

Wren carried on looking at the black screen. She chewed slowly like a dairy cow, with a look that let us know that the grass wasn't nearly sweet enough for her.

"Wren? Are you with us?" he said.

"Not by choice."

"Well, I'm waiting to show you something special."

"Here, I'll show *you* something special instead."

Slowly she raised her middle finger. She looked at it admiringly. I watched Dad's mouth tighten but knew he wouldn't explode. This was typical Wren. She was like a match with a huge phosphorous head that struck against any frictional surface it could find.

Dad wasn't going to do anything to help her ignite. You had to choose your battles very carefully.

I think Wren was born angry. She treated it like a natural talent that needed daily practice. The difference now was that the only people who had ever fought Wren and won—Floyd and our mum—weren't playing anymore.

Wren was Bellatrix Lestrange in looks and behavior, and Australia would be her Azkaban. She once said I was like Hermione without the brains. No prize for figuring out what that meant: without brains, Hermione was just plain annoying.

No one liked the way Wren made herself look and that suited her fine. She was anti-pretty and angry-beautiful, with overdrawn eyebrows and lips. If her makeup was designed to warn people away, her clothes were protective: a spiked choker, meshed sleeves, leather fingerless gloves, a chaos of black from head to steel-capped toe. Our neighbors glared at her as if she were about to feed on their young. She knew I was scared of her, but she didn't know that I admired her. It was hard not to care what people thought. We didn't look like sisters. I was a pale minikin with gossamer hair, a wisp of smoke. In old photos where I'm standing beside my brother and sister, I look like a hoax phantom.

Floyd had looked like he'd spent his whole life outdoors. He had been taller than Dad, fit and strong. He'd had dark honey waves that tumbled over one eye when he tilted his head to look at you. You'd do anything for him if he looked at you like that. (Usually, with me, it was taking over his dishwasher duties.) He had dark brown eyes that twinkled when he was being cheeky, tiny pinprick freckles on his nose, and a big smile. I'd thought of him as invincible.

The last mouthful of food turned sour on my tongue.

"Come on, Wren," said Dad. "You've been chewing that piece for five minutes."

Wren gave him the evil eye and let her plate drop to the coffee table with a loud clatter. Dad ignored the fuss, reached into the back pocket of his jeans, and produced a folded piece of paper, which he opened up precisely, like reverse origami.

First it went to Mum. She looked at it with the same tired, hollow look that she gave everything, and then she passed it to me.

It was a photograph of a house. Underneath was a long description that started with the words *"Sensationally positioned! The family home of your dreams."* Underneath that, Dad had written in his terrible handwriting *"24 Lime Street, Melbourne,"* and added an exclamation mark after it.

It was a gleaming white house made of horizontal boards and a shiny tin roof. There was a porch, two windows on either side of a black front door, and a perfectly round rose bush in front, like a face about to lick a pink lollipop.

On the porch was a wooden bench and three pairs of Wellington boots, large, medium, and small. Lavender poked through the gaps of the white fence.

It *was* lovely.

"You're speechless, hey?" said Dad.

"It doesn't look real." I was still angry about his plan and there was no way I actually wanted the stupid thing, but saying anything against this house would sound unconvincing.

"Give it to me." Wren snatched it away, and the paper sliced a minuscule line in the soft skin between my thumb and forefinger. She looked nuclear. Anyone with any sense would evacuate to the air-raid shelter.

But not Dad. He stood and held up another piece of paper: a photo of a puppy. A dark yellowish, scruffy one, lying on its tummy, its head resting on one tiny paw, its dark eyes full of longing.

"What's that?" Wren scowled.

"It's our dog." Dad's eyes were shining, desperate.

This was too much. I'd *always* wished for a dog. So had Floyd. We used to spend hours coming up with dog names, even though Dad had said there was absolutely no way we were getting one. Floyd's favorite name was Soda, after a character in a book he loved. I wanted something tough from mythology, like Hector or Juno. Getting one now was a betrayal.

"He's a golden retriever. A present for both of you. In Melbourne, waiting for us."

"We've got a cat, moron," said Wren. "Why the hell would we want a dog? Dogs are idiots."

Dad sighed. "But the cat . . . And *don't* call me a moron by the way."

33

"The cat *what?*"

"Nothing. The dog can be for Summer, then. Summer's always wanted one, haven't you?" He waved the paper in my direction. I had to take it.

It was no use. Hot tears started running down my cheeks, and there was nothing I could do to stop them.

"Typical!" Wren said with a growl. "Of course you'd side with Dad." She tried to screw up the picture she was holding and then rip it apart furiously, as if she couldn't decide the best way to destroy it, then she threw it at my head and hissed at me savagely on her way out of the room. Message received, Wren. Australia was as much my fault as Dad's. The injustice of it hurt but it was pointless to take her on. The hate in Wren wanted revenge and I was an easy target. A little blind larva wriggling between the tips of her beak.

I smoothed out the photo of the house on my right leg, put the hopeful puppy on my left, and silently told it to stop looking at me like that. Over my shoulder I sensed Mum looking. She hardly made a sound anymore. In the beginning that had been like the shock of someone switching off loud music at a party.

The picture-book house said "welcome." It was small. We wouldn't be able to hide from each other as much. It was also neat and new. I could almost smell the sour white paint and the soft musky flowers of the fat lavender bushes. I'd always wished for a porch with a bench, where I could sit and read books and watch people go by. The doors of this house would close properly, the floors wouldn't slope, and we'd never need to leave saucepans on the staircase when it rained.

But I'd never minded any of those faults. They were Jackman quirks, and they were special.

"Mum?" I said. "Do you want us to go?"

Mum pressed four fingers hard into her lips the way she always did when she was about to cry. It looked like the first part of a blown kiss.

Dad held out his hand over the arm of the sofa, but she didn't take it.

She said, softly, "Dad thinks . . ." and then swallowed the rest of the words before her face screwed up in pain. "Yes. Yes. Sorry." She squeezed my shoulder for an instant, but when I looked, her hand was back on her mouth, making me think I'd only imagined it.

After the bomb, the prime minister had gone on TV and said that we'd been lucky because only twelve people had died. Two of them were teenagers—Floyd and a girl we didn't know. The prime minister got into a lot of trouble in the papers for saying "lucky" and "only." But that was months ago. He'd have a whole bunch of new problems now. But we couldn't move on.

Mum slept and breathed and cried and that was all she could manage. She didn't look or sound or even smell the same. The doctors told Dad, who passed it on to me, that Mum had no choice. She wasn't behaving that way to hurt us.

But it did hurt.

Mum's name was Cecelia, which I thought was beautiful, but everyone called her Cece because it sounded more friendly. Once upon a time, Mum had been both of those things. She had been big and colorful and loud, a rainbow one day and a hurricane the next. You could hide behind her if you needed to, or she'd help you not to feel so shy if you let her. You could tell her your secrets and most of all you could trust her. She made things better.

She could be bossy, I suppose. Sometimes she used to snap at Dad if he was working too hard (which was often) or being boring (also, admittedly, often). If she had too much wine her temper could pop like a champagne cork. But honestly, that hardly ever happened.

This shell of Mum was doing silent crying with her mouth open and one fist clenched at her heart. She was all the pain in the world, and I felt numb, as if I was watching something too horrible for my brain to measure. I stared at the house on the paper and almost didn't notice her get up and squeeze my shoulder again as she left the room.

Dad and I were alone. When I looked, I saw he had tears in his eyes. I felt us nudge closer to his plan.

"To tell you the truth, I'm frightened for us, Summer. I want to take us somewhere new, better. I just want to protect us."

An uncomfortable pip stuck in my throat—the small, sharp-edged seed of the matter. If dads were frightened, what were the rest of us meant to do? *I* couldn't promise *him* that things would get better if we stayed. What did I know?

Softly, like the last bit of air in a balloon, I said, "Okay. We'll go."

His face brightened and he wiped his tears. It was that easy. All I had to look like was "okay," and all I had to say was "okay."

"You'll love it, Summer." He came to sit right next to me. "I guarantee it."

The room was so clogged up with other people's feelings that I couldn't work out my own. But Dad's plan was moving fast enough for things to go blurry and maybe that would feel better than the stiff, slow crawl of missing Floyd.

"Look at the photo of the house again, Summer. Tell me what you like about it."

He needed me back on his side, didn't he? "The Wellingtons," I said with my jaw clenched.

He nudged me playfully. "We say 'gumboots' in Oz." Then he put his arms around me, front and back, like safety bars on a fairground ride. We looked at the house together and my stomach lurched. I tried to imagine what lay outside the edges of the photograph. What the street would look like. How hot the sun would feel. Which birds we'd hear in the mornings. I remembered a song we used to sing at Girl Guides, the one about a laughing kookaburra. Laughing didn't feel right anymore.

Floyd had always wanted to go to Australia; he would have loved this. Mum had always wanted to go, too. They'd had exactly the same sense of adventure. We'd talked about living there before, but I'd always thought it was just pretend, like the talks we'd had about getting a dog or taking a year off school and caravanning around the world.

Maybe Dad was thinking that Mum would get better once we were far away. . . .

That was the thought that made me jump up and grab the phone as soon as it rang. It was Plan A calling.

"Mal, don't bother, it's just me."

"Er . . . Hello . . . I mean, *good evening*. This is Jamila Everdeen from the Australian Department of Immigration—"

"Mal, seriously, it's too late." On another day I'd have laughed at her mashed-up name—Jamila after one of her favorite authors, Everdeen after her favorite book character. She was going to try to convince Dad that there was a problem with our passports, to buy us time.

"Sorry, madam, I don't know who 'Mal' is. This is *Jamila Everdeen*. I wish to speak with Mr. Doug Jackman, please."

"Mal, stop. I mean it. We have to give up now."

It felt like forever until she spoke again.

"I don't know what I'll do without you, Summer."

She kept talking, and the nicer she was to me, the more I felt my heart getting smaller and colder. A china doll's tiny fist. Already I was forgetting how to talk to my best friend.

We hadn't even packed, but when I put the phone down, it was the end of something.

the other side of

laughter

It was Christmas Eve, and I was alone in the same spot where Dad had first told me we were leaving. Everything looked different. The treasures of our living room were gone. The rug had been rolled up and it leaned against the mantelpiece, full of our old footsteps. The curtains we'd hidden behind as little kids were slumped on the floor where the Christmas tree should have been. There would be no Christmas this year. We had four more days until we were leaving and that was our only countdown.

The house had changed and I'd changed, too. For a start, since around the time the Ibanez Artwood had come back, and especially when it was close to me, I'd had a visitor in my head.

—That's a strange thing to call me.

What are you, then? Actually, don't answer that.

Floyd sounded like more than a thought or a memory. I could hear his voice as clearly as if I had one earphone in and the volume down low. At first I'd been scared and wouldn't even admit to myself that it was really happening, but now I wanted him to stay.

—Look at this place! How can a room feel so empty with forty-three boxes crammed into it?

I know what you mean.

Floyd didn't like our old life packed up like this any more than I did, even though the boxes were stacked into forts like the ones he used to build for our games when I was little. Summer the princess, Wren the witch, and Floyd the brave knight.

Only, you're not here to defend me anymore.

—What did I always tell you? You don't need defending.

I didn't blame Floyd for what was happening to us. I didn't blame him for anything and never could. Even though he wasn't perfect, he was perfectly Floyd and he'd loved me exactly the way I was.

—And that's why you can't let me go.

Yes, that's why I won't let you go.

I'd been listening to Dad go on and on about Australia. No one else would. He'd been teaching me new words for things: a capsicum was a pepper, you colored in with a texta not a felt-tip pen, and there was an essential item called a rashie that you wore at the beach to stop sunburn.

Dad had bought us a jar of Vegemite. He said he'd grown up on it. He said all Australians loved it.

"Dad, I'm really sorry but this stinks," I'd said.

"Rubbish. Just try it. You put it on toast."

"I can't eat that."

"You'll be fine. Hold your nose."

Luckily for me he'd chosen that moment to read the ingredients and decided that Vegemite was deadly because of glutamates, whatever they were. He threw it out. For once Dad's health kick worked in my favor. But then I got worried: if I thought Vegemite was that horrible, and it was something all Australians loved, how was I ever going to fit in?

As well as going on about how perfect Australia was, Dad had started picking on our old life here. He pointed out everything that was wrong with our house, our suburb, the school we went to, and the weather. He said he'd always hated our street because it looked like no one cared. But I liked our street. All the houses were as rundown as one another. It was like staying in your pajamas all day with messed-up hair because you were with old friends and nobody cared what you looked like.

—What about that bright purple house at the end? Are you saying you like that one now?

Yes, I've changed my mind. It's . . . original.

It was no surprise that Wren had spent almost every waking hour since Dad had announced the move trying to sabotage it. She'd run away from home five times. The trouble was that she didn't exactly blend in, so Dad found her by combing the streets slowly in Dorrit (Mum's car), or the police picked her up. The fifth time, she'd taken the cat with her, but we found Charlotte mewing at the front door twelve hours after we'd discovered they were missing and an hour after that, Wren was home, too. She was even angrier that time than the times Dad or the police had found her.

Mum was still the same. Mostly she stayed in her room. Sometimes I'd go in and lie on the end of her bed with the cat, but I'd never look at Mum's face. I'd become too scared to do that. When she would leave—for the bathroom, or to wander around the house—I'd look around for clues about what she did in there all day long. The bookmark from the novel she was reading never moved, but the television was occasionally warm. Sometimes there would be half a mug of cold tea over by the windowsill. I kept telling myself that things were on hold until we left England, and not to worry too much.

The Ibanez Artwood was the thing keeping me going. It was propped against the side of the boxes along with a bunch of other things that didn't fit inside one: the cat basket, Mum's easel, and some framed school artwork by Floyd, Wren, and me. I reached over and took the guitar into my lap. The promise to keep it safe was still deep inside me, as tight as the strings that I still couldn't let my fingers go near. It was enough just to be close to it.

I tapped quickly and unevenly on the back of the guitar and looked into the sound hole. Floyd used to play a trick on me when I was little: he'd tap, just like I was doing now, and tell me there was a goblin inside who'd leap out and grab onto me with his dirt-caked fingernails if I ever took the guitar without permission.

—*You should have seen your face.*

Well, I was younger then. I believed in lots of impossible things. Anyway, that was a pretty mean thing you did.

—*You're shivering. Are you cold?*

Freezing.

—*So tell Dad.*

He's probably making it cold in here on purpose so he can keep going on about the benefits of Australia.

—*You know what I think? I think it wasn't the central heating that kept us warm all the years we lived here. It was all our stuff plugging up the cracks.*

Floyd was right. The cracks were everywhere.

Outside it was nighttime and freezing. It wouldn't be freezing in Australia. It would be tomorrow instead of today and everyone would be on the beach in their rashies. I tried to imagine myself in the blazing hot sun with all the carefree, happy people. It would feel like having the flu at a birthday party.

The doorbell rang, and I heard voices at the door. Mal and Deeta. I felt nervous and wished they hadn't come. It was easier to be alone with my thoughts and the guitar.

"I'd love to pop in and say a quick good-bye to Cece," I heard Deeta say.

Mum would be "in the bath" or "asleep" or "out." It didn't matter which excuse Dad used. I heard Deeta say good-bye to Dad but I knew Mal wouldn't leave with her. I waited for her to come into the living room.

It was such a strange feeling to like someone as much as I liked Mal and not want to see her. I'd stopped asking her to come over and I replied to her hundreds of messages with smiley faces. I'd run out of words. I couldn't stand this waiting. Every moment we spent together was a reminder of what I was going to miss.

But Mal wasn't easy to put off. She came into the room like a whirlwind.

"Wow, it looks huge in here! I can't believe how much you've done. Look at all these boxes!" She knelt down and hugged me. "Do you feel Christmassy? I don't. I wish it would snow. So look," she said, letting me out of the hug, "I bought some things to help get us in the mood." She held up a striped plastic bag I recognized from the corner shop. Then, between us, she placed a miniature Christmas pudding, two clementines with shiny green leaves still attached, two candy canes, and a packet of gingerbread stars with white icing.

"This is so nice," I said. I felt formal and awkward. I reached over the guitar and took a candy cane.

"So. How are you?" said Mal. She sounded like the school counselor.

"Okay." I shrugged.

"I haven't seen you for ages."

"We've been packing. Sorry."

"I could have helped."

She sounded hurt. I didn't know what to say. "We were fine. It was too boring to ask you to do it. Really."

By now we'd both sucked all the red out of the end of our candy canes. Mal looked like she was wearing lipstick. It made me wonder if the next time I saw her we'd have changed so much we'd hardly know each other.

"Tell the truth, Summer. Do you blame me?" Mal

said. Her voice had shifted from a happy major chord to a soft, sad minor chord.

"Blame you? For what?"

She put the colorless sticky end of the candy cane on the empty plastic bag. "I read online that people feel regret if they don't get to say goodbye to someone they love. And you were at my house when it happened."

I'd never seen Mal this close to tears. I was scared of how sad I'd made her without even knowing I was doing it.

"Of course I don't blame you, Mal." Because that would be horrible and pointless and something Wren might do. I was not like Wren at all . . . was I? "I don't, Mal. Seriously. Never."

"Okay. That's good." She grinned, believing me instantly. But I wondered if I believed myself.

Mal opened the packet of gingerbread stars. Then she peeled both clementines, dangled the peels from her ears as if they were earrings, and smiled goofily.

—*Give her something, Sum. Look at her. She's trying so hard.*

But I don't know what to say. And maybe I do blame her for that night. I could have been here with you.

—*Say anything.*

I took a deep breath and looked out the glass doors that led to the dark garden. And I saw something

47

beautiful. "Look, Mal, it's your wish!"

"It's snowing! Summer, it's actually snowing!"

We crawled excitedly to the glass doors and knelt there, looking out and up. I couldn't remember the last time it had snowed on Christmas Eve.

"The snow looks like fireflies," said Mal.

She was right. The snow was in flurries that tumbled frantically in midair. It was fast and muddled like a snow globe that can't settle.

"This might sound strange," I began, "but sometimes I think insects can travel between worlds."

"How come?"

"The way they move. One minute you see them, the next minute you don't. They disappear so fast— backward, even. Sometimes I imagine they've found tiny holes that lead to other universes."

"Wormholes?"

"You mean they exist? There's an actual name for them?"

We suddenly started to laugh.

"Do you have to be a worm to use them?" I squeaked.

We laughed like mad. We said silly things about worms. We didn't care. This was exactly the sort of conversation I'd only ever had with Mal. My head was filled with nothing but our laughter, and I never wanted it to stop.

the other side of
the room

As I was going up to bed that night, I heard Dad in the cellar. We'd already cleared it so I went down to see what he was doing.

At the bottom of the steps I froze. Dad was standing with his back to me, his hands clasped behind his neck. He was facing Floyd's old skateboard ramp. The only thing left. I remembered the day Floyd had made it in the back garden. Dad had shouted at him for using a piece of skirting board that he'd been meaning to nail back into place "one of these days."

My foot made the stair creak, and Dad turned around. The despair on his face vanished and he smiled, as if he could change channels just like that.

"Nearly done here!" he said cheerily.

"That's good, Dad."

I felt so bad for him. It was Dad's job to decide what to do with that ramp.

—*The new kids might like it.*

Wouldn't you mind?

—*It was the best quarter pipe I ever made. Deserves to be used.*

"Dad?" I said. "We should leave it for the next family that lives here."

This time his smile looked real. "That's a great idea, sweetheart."

I turned back around then. At the top of the cellar stairs I noticed a scar on the wall that I'd never seen before. I put my fingertip to one end and let it glide through the deep groove to the other. All the marks in this house had a story but this was one story I hadn't heard before. Now I never would.

———————

Dad had promised Wren and I separate bedrooms in Melbourne. He was smart, despite what Wren thought of him. If we'd stayed here, I don't think even Wren would ever have been able to move into Floyd's room, despite how much she was always saying that she hated sharing with me. (Dad had packed up Floyd's room on his own. It hadn't been discussed. I hadn't even asked what he'd done with Floyd's other guitar in case I didn't like what I heard.)

Two years ago Wren had rigged up some tie-dyed sheets on a piece of string to divide our bedroom in half. That still wasn't enough. She'd sigh when my *shadow* got on her nerves. Our bedroom was a battleground. As usual, I had the Ibanez Artwood with me for backup, propped in the corner on my side of the room.

We both had single mattresses on the floor now. Dad had sold the beds on eBay along with almost every other piece of furniture we owned.

Wren's side of the room used to look like the Chamber of Horrors. She'd say that my side looked like unicorn vomit. Both sides looked the same now: bare walls with shiny circles where the Blu-Tack had taken the paint away.

"What are you doing with that guitar all the time?" Wren's voice shot through the small gap between the sheets.

"Looking after it."

She scoffed, and I knew there'd be more.

"Could you *not* spray that disgusting stuff everywhere?"

"It's deodorant, Wren. Leave me alone."

"You're getting into bed. Why do you need to smell like a meadow?"

—Don't rise to it. You know she can't help it.

How come she gets to be the angry one?

Through the gap, I spied Wren curled up with Charlotte, the cat she named after a spider. Charlotte was small and black with surprising patches of orange fur in three spots, like when you tear off a piece of wall-paper and find the old wallpaper underneath. Wren and Charlotte were in a huge nest made of all the clothes she'd wrenched out of Dad's hands earlier when he'd tried to pack them into one of the forty-three boxes. There were dozens of black tights, long skirts, and lace-up ankle boots. For someone who had so many clothes and acces-sories that we couldn't take them in a suitcase, it was impressive that she looked the same every day.

—That's more like it. You can give as good as you get, you know.

Yes, but only inside.

"Stop looking at me through the gap, you little freak."

"Fine! God, what's *up* with you?"

"You! Why'd you have to be so helpful to Dad? How can you even bear to be on his side? I'm not going to Australia, you know."

"Good! Whatever! Don't, then!"

—Um, Summer? You need to work on your comebacks.

"I know, Wren, why don't you try running away again? That seemed to go really well for you."

"Shut up, you moronic midget."

Ouch. One of Mum's old sayings came to me: don't dish it out if you can't take it. I couldn't. I slid under the covers and stewed. I didn't want to go to Australia any more than she did. I *could* be just as angry as she was, but Wren owned being a human volcano.

"I will literally die there," she said. "I'll die. DIE! Of the heat, the beaches, the cheeriness, the idiot kangaroos bouncing all over the stupid place."

I wanted to laugh but didn't dare. Sometimes she was so angry it actually came out funny.

—*She's scared. You know that, right?*

Fine. You win, Floyd. I'll be nice.

"Kangaroos can't kill you, Wren. It's just a normal country full of normal things." I hoped.

"What's that supposed to mean? Shut up. I hate you, Summer. It's going to be like *Home and Away*."

This was obviously not the time to mention that I quite liked *Home and Away*. She was impossible.

"We're going to be so far away. From everything." Wren's voice had softened, as if the real her had slipped out of the room.

"I know."

"Then why the *hell* aren't you angry about it?" she yelled.

My eyes and nose prickled. I *was* angry! I had so

many feelings but hers suffocated mine. I could only scream and yell silently. Both of us had drawn a chalk circle on the ground around our feet—she was angry Wren, I was timid Summer—and who knew what would happen if we stepped outside?

"You hate everything in the whole world," I said, the cracks starting to show in my voice. "Why do you care which bit of it we live in?"

"Oh, don't start crying, you idiot. I don't hate *every-thing*. Just Dad."

I held my breath.

"And you."

"Great. Thanks a lot." I cried as quietly as I could.

—*Listen to me. She doesn't mean it, Sum.*

You don't know that. And you don't even know how it feels—she loved you. Everyone loved you.

I wiped my snotty nose on the edge of the duvet. "Dad thinks Mum might get better in Australia," I said.

"Mum's never getting better. She's been sucked into a black hole and it's one-way only. I wish I could get sucked in there with her. You can stay in Happy Land with Dad."

I knew that Wren liked to think that she had Mum and I had Dad, but the truth was that no one had Mum anymore.

We were quiet then, and my cheeks were tight

where the tears had dried. I looked through the gap. Wren had her big headphones on and the ceiling was getting a dirty look.

My eyes were just closing when I heard knuckles rapping on the door.

"Girls?" Dad popped his head in. He looked nervously at my sister. "I need that music system, Wren."

She didn't move a muscle.

Dad took a breath. "Wren! TURN IT OFF."

"WHAT?" Half a smile, pretending she couldn't hear.

"TAKE THE HEADPHONES OFF."

"WHAT?"

"I'VE ASKED YOU ALL DAY, WREN!"

"WHAT?"

"FOR GOD'S SAKE!" Dad reached down to the socket and yanked out the plug. "Listen to me. It has to go on the ship with everything else. I'm running out of time! Doesn't anyone understand?"

Poor Dad, standing there yelling at us with the end of the long wire clenched in his fist and the plug flopping over as if it were the head of a snake blacked out from his squeezing. He went on yelling about how it was all on him—*all on him*—and I didn't like being put in the same basket as Wren and Mum. I *had* been helping. I *was* trying. He was sweating and getting redder, and veins bulged from his neck.

Through the gap I saw Wren stagger to her feet. As she scooped up her stereo, the cat shot out the door in between Dad's legs. Time seemed to slow down. Wren's face glowed with rage. She steadied herself on the mattress, twisted her body around, and then hurled the stereo toward Dad with a scream that sounded like her throat was ripping apart.

Dad cried out as it flew in his direction and landed against him. I felt it, too, how hard it would have dug into the soft flesh on the inside of his arms. There was a flicker of despair in his face, but I think the shock had silenced him, and he hugged the stereo, breathing heavily.

Wren flopped down on her bed and curled away from me to face the wall. The room thrummed with her anger. But Dad had calmed down and was trying to look like someone who'd gotten exactly what he came for.

"Nearly there," he said, maybe only to himself. "'Night, girls."

"'Night, Dad."

Half of me still hated Dad and his plan, but the other half understood why he thought we had to do this. I missed the way I used to love him: simple and endless, like a cloudless sky. Maybe I could be bigger than I felt I was. I stretched out of my bed to put my face near the gap.

"I'm sorry, Wren." I didn't really know what I was sorry for but it was worth a shot. "Merry Christmas."

There was no reply.

In the dark, I felt alone. Apparently there were seven stages of grief but that was a neat way of putting it. Grief was messy and didn't color inside the lines. I could switch from one to the other. I could feel all seven in a day. This felt like number four: despair.

Then I thought of the Ibanez Artwood. I got out of bed and sat with it on the floor in a ribbon of moonlight that ran across the carpet. The guitar was cold against my bare legs and the strings were silvery.

—*An object like this isn't just for looking at, Summer.*

I can't play it, Floyd. It's yours. It's you.

—*One chord at a time. Just trust me, okay? I'm still your big brother.*

He was right. This guitar had to be more than an ornament to have survived the way it had. I took a deep breath and held it in. Middle finger high E, second fret. Index finger on the G, second fret. Ring finger on the B, third fret. My thumb grazed the strings to play the softest D.

That night I found myself standing in the space where Floyd's bed had been. My legs were ice-cold and stiff.

I must have been sleepwalking again. I stayed still and tried to remember the dream that had brought me here. It was this:

I hear chords from a song Floyd had been working on for weeks. It's the one that he told me he couldn't finish. This song had never sounded right to him but he couldn't explain why and he couldn't let it go.

I tiptoe silently toward the sound, dream-thinking that he's come back to us. I'm scared to be wrong but can't stop the hope rapidly expanding in my heart like a time-lapse flower.

I open the door and see him on his bed with his back to me, holding his guitar. He's going over and over the same part, humming where there are no words. His hair jolts on each chord. I see the angle of his jawline and the bristles that have started to grow there. He's so real, and so close.

Suddenly I know what the missing line should be. I try to sing it to him but no sound comes out. So I walk over and tap my brother on the shoulder.

And when he turns around, he has a completely different face.

the other Side of
quiet

I was glad to leave our house. Being there at the end was like kicking it when it was down. It was lifeless, like the fixed eyes of the rats Charlotte used to catch and leave for Mum on the back doorstep. Eyes that said "I give up." It was hard to imagine it had been our noisy home.

We couldn't leave England without first going to Gran's house, near Tintagel in Cornwall, two hundred and fifty miles from London, in a wild open space. Dad drove us all there in Dorrit. I loved that blue-gray Morris Minor. Mum had bought it when she was at university and, despite lots of breakdowns, she had never given up on it. It had beautiful curves over the wheels and big round headlights and wing mirrors. There was a square boot with a wooden frame, and double doors at the back that were hinged on the sides, which together made it look more like a small, cozy room than the back of a car. In there we had four large pieces of luggage and the Ibanez Artwood, tucked up safely in the velvet-lined case. I hadn't played it for a few days, or thought very hard about why. The face from the dream and the line from the song were unreachable to me now.

—*You know what I'm about to say, don't you?*

I won't get perfect calluses if I don't practice every day? I know, Floyd. I will.

It would take days of practice before my fingertips were tough enough again that each chord wouldn't sting. I'd built them up before, when Floyd used to give me lessons, and I would do it again once we got to Australia. I'd have no friends and nothing else to do, so I was going to put everything into the Ibanez Artwood.

On the drive we were quiet, but I thought I could sense something different between Mum and Dad. He wasn't making his usual effort to talk to her, and she had a new look on her face that I could just make out if I pressed my cheek into the car window and caught her reflection in the sideview mirror. She looked steely.

Maybe it was the thought of seeing Gran. They battled as often as Dad and Wren.

Gran seemed like part of nature. She was different from London people. She had strength in her arms, the weather in her face, and dirt under her fingernails.

—*I can taste Gran's bread already. Have double for me, Sum.*

Floyd, don't joke. I wish you were here so much it hurts.

—*Sorry, I can't help it. The atmosphere in this car is so . . .*

I know.

Finally, in the dark, we passed the sign for Gran's village. Everyone stirred and stretched and I wound down my window. Already I could hear animal sounds I could never hear in London because of the traffic. I looked up. The sky seemed enormous.

We piled out of the car outside Gran's. The wind was an extra-strong mint in my brain, wiping away all traces of the motorway fumes and the weird atmosphere of the journey. The sea air in Cornwall let you know who was in charge. Tintagel was a place where the elements seemed stronger than anything human. I liked that. Humans had a choice and you could drive yourself mad trying to understand why they kept destroying one another. But nature was different and I didn't believe it caused damage on purpose.

When Gran came out of the house and walked down

her front path with open arms, I think we all knew that she meant to welcome the four of us, but Dad, Wren, and I stood back while Mum ran into the hug.

"Now, then. That's better," said Gran.

Nobody moved for a while. It was just the wind, the darkness, and my mum being comforted by hers.

After we'd carried the luggage inside, Gran fed us cheese sandwiches I could hardly get my jaw around, with homemade white bread and almost as much butter as cheese. Dad didn't argue. They were delicious. Then she told us all to go to bed, and nobody argued with that, either.

Wren and I were on narrow single beds at either end of a long room. Although the air in there was wintry, I knew the beds would be toasty. Gran had flask-shaped ceramic hot water bottles that were even older than she was. The mattresses were as soft and deep as cake, with layers of sheets and blankets tucked in so tightly that we could only get under them by sliding in from the top. The marshmallow pillows cupped my head, and Mum even came in to say goodnight.

When Mum was sitting on Wren's bed, I could hear my sister talking in a way that made her sound little again. I got a sprinkling of feeling that happiness was almost in reach. Mum's replies to Wren were low and quiet like a violin bow pulled along the deepest string.

Then it was my turn. Mum sat so close to me that the covers tightened uncomfortably, but I wasn't going to say a word about that.

"It's nice here," I whispered, so that it could be just between us. Mum nodded and smiled. She kissed me on the cheek and rested her head on the pillow. The tip of her nose grazed my ear, and I could feel her breathing me in. I only cared about Mum and me in that moment.

When she sat up, she traced her thumb over my forehead. I wanted to tell her that we should stay here in Cornwall instead of going to Melbourne, but I didn't want to make her sad again.

I lay awake for a while afterward. It was darker and quieter here but it wasn't lonely like home. Gran's house felt like it was the boss of us. It told us that we could go to sleep inside it and trust that everything would be okay in the morning. I drifted off peacefully.

———

Over breakfast the next morning—the morning before our last morning—Gran let something slip.

"Charlotte looks like she's settled in already, so you don't need to worry, girls. I know you've been particularly fond of her, Wren, dear."

Dad started coughing, obviously fake. I knew what Gran meant straightaway but Wren didn't get it. We weren't taking Charlotte with us, but they hadn't wanted to tell us. I didn't know what to feel, but that almost didn't matter because Wren was going to feel it all.

"Charlotte can settle anywhere," said Wren. "Even Australia if she has to. I'm going to train her to kill possums."

"Don't say that. What did possums ever do to you?" I don't know why that came out of my mouth. Possums were beside the point. Any minute now, Wren was going to rain hell down on all of us. Charlotte was her best friend.

"Possums look like rats with marbles for eyes," she went on, still oblivious. "Charlotte's going to devour their brains."

Gran poured more tea from the pot and gave Dad a stern look. But it was Mum who spoke to Wren.

"Charlotte's staying here, darling."

"What?" Wren stabbed the table with the end of her spoon. "What are you talking about?"

Mum went on. "Charlotte's old, Wren. She wouldn't do well on the flight. It would be cruel to make her go. She needs to stay with Gran."

It was so new hearing Mum talk this much that I was mesmerized. She sounded calm—different from the old Mum, but in control. I knew that Wren was going to kick off now and make life horrible for hours, but seeing Mum like this made me think that I'd been right to hope that things would get better. Even when Wren screamed and threw her cereal bowl at the wall and told us she wished we were all dead while the milk ran down in rivers.

She took the cat from her bed by the fire. I heard the tiny rip of claws losing their grip on the cushion, as if Charlotte was trying to tell Wren that she really wanted to stay here with Gran. Wren draped Charlotte over her shoulder like a stole as she left the kitchen. Dad had his face in his hands. Mum's face and Gran's, too, were stony as they cleared the dishes and wiped the milk from the wall.

But I was okay. I'd miss Charlotte, but having Mum back was better than a cat. Finally it was looking like Dad's plan wasn't so stupid after all.

———

We were a different sort of quiet in Gran's house and it was the good sort. The house was so crammed full of things to look at and you could always hear the wind and the waves outside. Things were simpler here.

—I spent one whole summer here by myself, remember?

Of course I do. I missed you. I think I drove Mum mad asking her every single day when you'd be back. Then finally you were, and you'd grown heaps and you could play the guitar like a pro.

—That's all I did the whole time I was here.

That's all I'll do when we get to Melbourne.

Mum curled up with a book in a huge squashy armchair by the fire. She hadn't cried since we left London. Maybe our house had been too full of memories. She was wearing a big gray cardigan of Gran's that made her look safe and small inside. I liked watching Gran take care of her, and Mum letting Gran do it. The way they used to argue felt like something I'd imagined.

In the afternoon, while Wren was soaking off her rage in Gran's enormous claw-foot bath, I took Charlotte into my lap and sat in the window seat at the porthole in the bedroom.

All houses should have a round window you can sit inside, but unfortunately not all of them would have a view like this: a distant cliff top, an endless messy sea of sparkling grays and indigos, even a soaring kestrel. It was a picture that could make you believe in impossible things.

Charlotte had fallen into a blissful sleep as I stroked her behind her ears the way she liked. This was our good-bye, and it hurt. But didn't Wren, with her crying and denial, make her pain worse? We could have a completely new life in Australia. I could be brave and say some more good-byes.

Good-bye, old house. Good-bye, old life. Good-bye, old friends.

Whoever got Mal would be the lucky one. But I couldn't take our friendship with me. I needed portable, solid, dependable things, like the Ibanez Artwood.

The next time I opened the case, we'd all be somewhere new.

the other side of
good-byes

On the morning of our flight, Gran made coddled eggs with cream, and thick buttered toast on the side. It was only Dad and Gran and I eating because Wren had locked herself in the bathroom with Charlotte and Mum was still sleeping.

"Shouldn't I wake her?" I said.

"Not yet. Leave her," said Dad, getting up from the table. He was twitchy. He'd left to check the passport folder three times already.

"It'll be all right, Doug," said Gran firmly. She patted his chair and he sat down again. She poured him more tea from her pot, which was big enough to fit a cat inside (we had tried once when we were little), and stirred in three sugars. Dad seemed to have forgotten his health kick and no one was rushing to remind him.

"Right. Time to sort out your sister," said Gran. She took off her apron and left the kitchen. I wished Gran was coming to Melbourne with us. Nothing felt as safe as the way it did when we were with her. Yesterday's stack of unafraid good-byes might fall over if I put Gran on top.

Gran got my sister out of the bathroom, but Wren's face was like thunder. She kept picking up the cat from the fireplace and hugging her so tightly the poor thing looked like her eyes were about to pop out. And then Charlotte would jump down and go straight back to the squashy velvet cushion Gran had put down by the potbelly stove. Charlotte wanted to stay and I think that made Wren even angrier.

"I'm going to wake Mum," Wren said, in a break from chasing Charlotte.

"Wait," said Gran sternly, grabbing Wren's arm. "This is my house and I say when folks are woken up."

Wren blushed and huffed and finally slumped into an ancient armchair with a seat so low that only her head was visible.

Dad and I were restless. He unzipped the luggage and zipped it back up, and I went to the bathroom four times. Gran said "Nerves" every time she saw me come out. She was keeping herself busy with her thick arms deep in a mixing bowl, kneading dough for fresh bread. I couldn't help thinking that we wouldn't be here long enough to eat it. Wren got up from her chair and she and I stood on either side of Gran, picking at the raw dough with our fingers. Gran scolded us in her funny, gruff way.

"You two are getting under my feet. I want you both to go out for a walk. Now. Off you go."

"But it's freezing out there!" said Wren.

That was true. There was condensation on Gran's kitchen window.

"Do as I say, young madam. It's time. Time I got this bread in, for one. Isn't it, Doug?" Gran's face was serious but she grabbed Wren into a big hug and then pulled me in, too. She had the smell of someone who lit fires every day.

"Do I *have* to go with Summer?" said Wren, her head so close to mine that I could feel her breath on my cheek. "Can't we just go for a walk separately?"

"Stop pretending to be so awful, Wren," said Gran. She let us go and we straightened up. "I don't buy it for a moment. I mean it, my girl. Enough. Floyd wasn't one to sulk, was he? He'd have told you."

I couldn't tell what Wren was thinking in that moment, but her painted eyebrows were drawn together in a frown. We hardly ever said Floyd's name out loud.

Gran hadn't finished. "And look after Summer—and yourself, for that matter—or you'll have me to answer to."

Wren sighed deeply. "Fine, Gran. I promise to try very hard not to push her off a cliff."

"Well done. And Summer, as for you . . . well, you're a big girl now. That's all."

"Yes, Gran."

"Good girls. Head for the village, not the beach. That's the safest walk. Now off with you."

"Charming," Wren said. "Come on then, squirt." She almost sounded as if she couldn't be bothered to be mean. It was amazing what Gran could do.

We walked on opposite sides of the road. Everyone we passed said hello, but they were nice, normal hellos because nobody in Tintagel knew about Floyd and felt sorry for us. Gran was famous in the village for her garden and for some of her political campaigns, but she said that none of them really knew the first thing about her and that's the way she preferred it. She was like a really smart celebrity in that way.

The villagers even smiled at Wren, and the look on her face made me start to laugh.

"What's so funny?" she said.

71

A car passed between us and gave me time to lose the grin. "Nothing. I was just thinking about something else and your face happened to be in the way."

For once I had the last word.

We'd been walking for twenty minutes when Dorrit passed us and slowed to a stop. Dad was driving. Gran had probably sent him on an errand to get him out of her way, just like she'd sent us on the walk.

"Get in, girls," Dad said when we reached him. His eyes were bloodshot.

"What for? Gran told us to go walking," said Wren.

"Could you just do as you're told for *once*, Wren?"

His tone made me jump. I didn't need to be told twice and neither, apparently, did Wren. She took the front seat and I got in behind her.

"Seat belts."

"Dad, it's a country road and we're only two minutes from Gran's house."

"I said SEAT BELTS!"

"All right, keep your wig on."

"Wren! For God's sake!" He looked as if he was about to go on shouting but he stopped suddenly. He put his hand on Wren's shoulder. Then he faced forward and started the engine.

The atmosphere in the car thrummed in my bones like a deep bass note.

"Dad," I said nervously, "don't get angry but we're going in the wrong direction. Gran's house is back that way."

"It's all right, Summer."

My back pressed into the seat as the car sped up.

"What's going on?" said Wren.

"I need you to be really brave and good now, girls."

"Why? What do we need to be brave about?" she demanded.

"I'm going to tell you. Just give me a moment. I need to concentrate on driving."

Instinctively I put my hand to my chest where my heart was running itself to panic. "Dad, tell us quickly. You're scaring me." I could see the side of his face from the back seat. He was clenching his stubbled jaw, and the muscles of his face twitched like creatures hiding under sand.

"Everything's fine, girls. Please just wait a second. I need to focus."

The car sped up a little more, still going in the wrong direction. Wren started shouting at Dad in her usual way. I watched us join a main road and turned to look out of the back window, just as a fierce rain came pelting down. Somewhere back there was Gran and Mum and Charlotte. That's when I noticed our luggage in the trunk and, instantly, everything inside me hurt.

"I know what it is," I said. "Wren, she's not coming with us."

"Who? The cat? I know that, you idiot!"

I couldn't breathe. I saw the whole morning in fast forward from a new perspective. Mum not showing for breakfast. The stony silence between her and Dad in the car on the way here. Mum so happy to be with Gran. Gran getting us out of the way. Had they planned this or had Mum decided at the last minute?

"Are either of you mutants going to tell me what the hell is going on?" shouted Wren.

"Dad, say it," I said, still hoping I'd had the wrong idea.

Dad kept his eyes on the road, but his face was full of pain.

I was right.

"What is it?" Wren looked around at me and then at Dad.

"Dad, say it," I said again, louder.

"You say it, Summer!" screeched Wren. "Someone tell me!"

I started to cry. It came out as a high-pitched moan. "Mum."

"Oh my God. You mean we're going without her," said Wren. "YOU MEAN MUM!"

My eyes were swimming with tears as Wren raged

on, madly twisting under her seat belt as she shouted at the window.

"I don't understand!" she shouted at the top of her voice. "How could she not come with us?" Wren thumped the window with her fist and kicked the dashboard. And then she said, softer, as if the shock was setting in, "You mean she just isn't coming today, Dad? She's getting a different flight? What do you mean? Tell me! You have to tell me!"

"IT'S JUST FOR TODAY!" Dad yelled. All our different cries and gasps for breath filled the car; there was no air. Dad continued, steadier now. "She needs time with Gran. Just for a while. I begged her. Believe me, I begged her to come."

"Just for today? Or just for a while? Or longer? Which is it?"

"I don't know, Wren!"

Wren started screaming again. "Why didn't we say good-bye? How could you do this?" This time she sounded like a wild animal, with her hands like claws and her teeth bared. No words, just a sound. Her scream was my scream. I sat in stunned silence. It was the language of loss and, most of all, disbelief that the pain we thought we had been dealing with had grown a new tumor. Wren didn't believe it was just for a while any more than I did.

The empty seat beside me was like a sinkhole. The doctors said Mum couldn't control how she felt, but *this* felt like something she'd chosen. And I could taste how angry I was. It made me shake everywhere, from my fingers to my back teeth. I pressed my cheek to the cold window because I thought I might faint. From there I saw Wren's face in the round sideview mirror where two days ago I'd seen Mum's. Wren cried messily and I stared.

Then all I could hear was the road and Wren's ragged breathing, until she said, in a tight squeak that stuck in my heart, "But . . . she's our mum."

"I'm so sorry," said Dad. "But you, me, and Summer— we've got everything else we need."

That's when I checked the boot again and saw what else was missing. There was no guitar case. I gasped, and then tears spilled quickly and quietly down my face as if a completely new supply had been found. No Ibanez Artwood. I felt a pain that was so new it hurt twice as much. But I couldn't say it out loud—"How could you forget the guitar, Dad? I can't live without it."— because it was impossible to explain what it meant not to have an object when we'd just found out that we were missing our mum.

The hard Cornish rain somehow knew its job. It did its best to drown out the sound of our hearts breaking.

And the long road continued; it didn't know or care about our troubles.

It was taking us away from everything we'd ever known.

part two

AUSTRALIA

the other side of the World

Before sad things have happened to you, and you've only heard about them happening to other people, it's hard to imagine how people get through it. But the truth is that it's hard to understand even when it's your turn.

For a whole day and night, with a quick stopover in Hong Kong, Dad and Wren and I sat in a row, facing forward, not talking about Mum. We ate four meals—including a packet of mints and an ice-cold banana when they'd turned the lights out and it seemed like I was the only person on the plane who was awake—not talking about Mum. We watched safety demonstrations and movies, gave the crew our drink orders, and politely climbed over one another to walk to the toilets. To anyone else we probably looked normal.

Now the cabin crew marched up and down the aisles, getting us ready for landing, and none of this felt like something I was getting through. I was on a plane that someone else was flying, and that's what my life felt like, too.

The plane dipped. I gulped the swollen feeling from my ears. I looked at Dad looking at the view and wondered if he was thinking "home." But I pushed that thought away for a new, angry thought to grow: if Dad hadn't made us come here, we'd still be four. If Mum had tried harder, Dad would never have come up with this plan in the first place. Hating them both was soft and unsure at the moment, like the delicate top of a half-baked sponge cake. But I wanted the hate. I was finished with other people's feelings.

The cabin crew took their seats. It looked like the land was coming up to meet the plane as much as we were falling toward it. A few people cheered when the wheels touched the runway. I turned around to see them—a group on an adventure. Their smiles looked like a foreign language. I felt smaller than ever, and completely defeated. The ground under us was a hard and heavy truth.

The engine noise stopped. Seat belts clicked apart.

"Here," Wren said, handing me my bag from the overhead locker. It was only then that I realized how long it had been since she'd sniped at me. Twenty-three hours, to be precise.

We sweltered, quietly, waiting in line for a taxi. Wren's pale face turned pink and the tiny hairs around her hairline curled with sweat. She stripped off black layer after black layer until her pale arms showed. Dad had shadows under his eyes. He caught me looking but he didn't seem to be able to look back for very long. My eyes were full of gravel.

The taxi driver, Dave, was so friendly that we all had to grin back and pretend we felt something like normal. But the smile felt wrong on my face, the way your skin feels when you wash it with soap and it gets so tight.

"So where've you just come from, folks? You on holiday here?"

"London," said Dad in a lifeless voice. "But we thought we'd try a new life, didn't we, girls?"

"Good on ya, mate!" said Dave.

Hearing his accent was like watching Australian soaps on TV. I couldn't believe I was actually *in* this scene instead of back home in my school uniform, watching it with Mal.

It was the middle of the night back home. Mal would be asleep. Would Mum be sleeping, too? I gulped and bit the inside of my mouth to stop the tears. The pain made me angry, and anger was easier to deal with right now.

"I went to Leeds once," said Dave. "I've got family there. Do you know the place?"

"Not really," said Dad.

"Right, mate, right. You watch cricket? See the T20 last week? We gave you a hiding."

"I don't really follow it, to be honest." Dad sounded too tired for words.

"Soccer?"

"Not soccer either." Dad smiled weakly and then turned his head to stare out of the front passenger window. In the rearview mirror I caught Dave raising his eyebrows. Australia 1, Britain 0.

We whizzed over a bridge and a neat city popped out of the distance on our left. I thought, if we just keep moving, I'll be okay. First I hadn't wanted the plane to land and now I didn't want the car to stop. All I could see was this enormous sky towering over my head, making me feel like a tiny dot of raw hurt among millions of other tiny dots. My head said, "Look, the sky is beautiful!" But my heart said, "Listen, the world is enormous and you are only just beginning to understand what pain is. The way it clings to your body, like this heat."

Dad and Wren and I got out of the taxi at 24 Lime Street. "*Sensationally positioned! The family home of your dreams.*" The picture was right in front of us now. Dad opened the mailbox and took out an envelope with his name on it. Here was the key. It was all so surreal. We went inside quickly as if we'd finally found a place to hide.

Outside had been so hot and bright. Inside was dim and quickly filled with a dry and noisy cool from the air conditioner that Dad had switched on. The house echoed all our movements. We paced and stared. The journey to get here had taken weeks and now it was over. We were really in the *here* that had once been *there*.

A small hallway with two closed doors led into an open-plan kitchen and lounge. The whole place was empty, but not empty like our old house had felt at the end. I didn't feel sad for this one because this emptiness had nothing to do with us; it was someone else's.

"I'm going for a sleep, girls. You should, too. This one's mine." Dad pointed to one of the doors off the hallway.

His bedroom was already "mine" and not "ours" like his and Mum's in London had been. Now that we were here, I wasn't sure that Mum was ever coming.

"New mattresses were delivered the other day, the landlord said. We'll sort the rest out later."

The way Dad looked, I guessed that "later" could be days away.

There were glass doors all the way along the lounge room and, behind them, a neat, empty garden with a lemon tree in one corner, a large rectangle of patchy grass, and high fences all the way around. Suddenly I remembered the promised dog. When were we supposed to pick it up? I couldn't face asking Dad about it. A dog was the last thing I needed.

Wren wheeled her suitcase across the polished floors but at the foot of the stairs she suddenly stopped. "Are you coming up, then?"

She was different. Odd. This was the longest a cease-fire had lasted, just when I felt like I had enough anger to finally match hers.

Upstairs was twenty degrees hotter, with lower ceilings and harder edges, stark white walls, and rough blue carpet lining the short hallway.

There was a small window in the middle of the hall, with a view of the garden, and beyond that a church steeple and lots of trees that looked a bit like the ones we had at home. I'd expected gum trees and koalas, to be completely honest, but I kept that to myself.

To the right there was a bedroom. I followed Wren inside. It was like a giant white cube with wooden floors. A mattress that looked like it wanted to burst out of its plastic wrapping was propped against one wall.

"Summer, you've got your own room across there."

"Right. I forgot."

"I'm going to sleep for a bit. See you later. Um . . . sleep well."

Definitely weird. I went to the identical room across the hallway.

Empty.

I pulled the mattress down from the wall. It landed with a great thud that shook my bones. I wanted to smash something or just make a noise, but there was nothing else in the room. I kicked the wall with the heel of my shoe and made a black mark, the only scar in this perfect space. I tore the plastic off the mattress until my fingers hurt.

By the time I'd finished, I'd moved past tired into dizzy and confused. The room was too bright and we were in Australia.

Australia?

Australia.

Abracadabra.

It sounded as ridiculous as when Dad had first told me, but now we were actually in it and so far from everything except the pain.

Awake.

Awake.

The word was a dripping tap.

Awake.

Awake.

Awake.

Mal would be wondering about me, waiting for an email or a call. I could never tell her that Mum hadn't come. I was so ashamed and I couldn't have kind, hopeful Mal persuading me not to be angry or trying to convince me that, deep down, Mum loved me.

I shut Mal and Mum and everyone else out of my mind.

Please let me sleep, I thought. Let me not be here and not have these thoughts anymore.

Finally my eyelids were closing. My eyes were dry and prickly and sore from tears. Inside my head became quiet and empty. Without Floyd's guitar, I knew I wouldn't hear his voice. He was gone, like the end of a day, and for the second time I hadn't even said good-bye.

the other side of
twelve

A sound bounced off the bare walls. A doorbell. *Our* doorbell? I'd never heard it before. It was an electronic ding-dong sound and nothing like the sharp sleighbell one we used to have. I was upstairs in bed but heard it as clearly as if I had been standing in the downstairs hall. Everything was louder in an empty house.

The three of us had been on different planets since we'd arrived; awake, asleep, and hungry at different times. I'd heard Wren in the shower in the middle of the night. More than once I thought I'd seen Dad standing in my doorway, watching me sleep. But in the white light of morning I would wonder if he'd really been there. Jet lag had muffled all my feelings, and the days and nights were running loose, like something we'd spilled.

The times I'd gone downstairs to find food, Dad's door had been closed. There was white bread, margarine, milk, and pre-sliced cheese in the fridge, a little less every time I looked. I felt like a Borrower, scratching around completely unnoticed. I'd folded flat squares of cheese into my mouth and eaten white bread separately, wishing it could be comforting cheese on toast but not willing to try the cold, unused grill. Dad obviously hadn't found a health-food shop yet. Or maybe he'd left all that behind, too.

The doorbell ringing was the first sign that life had noticed we'd been holed up in here for days. Now, in bed, I stared at the ceiling, wondering if Dad or Wren would answer the door. Then I sat bolt upright, switched on by a thought that should have been the first thing on my mind. Today wasn't just an ordinary day of the week. *Today* was . . . Well, today might mean the doorbell was for me. My heart inflated like a balloon given one sudden puff of air.

The doorbell rang again. I grabbed some shorts and nearly fell over in my rush to get my legs inside. What if it was Mum? What if she'd really come after all? Today of all days, which would be perfect.

I stopped at the top of the stairs when I heard Dad

call out, "Coming!" That was when doubt bloomed in my chest. Was that the voice he'd use if it were Mum? And . . . wait, wouldn't Dad have told us she was landing this morning? Wouldn't he have picked her up from the airport?

But still, today was . . .

I ran down the stairs and flung myself around the corner and through the living room until I arrived breathlessly in the hallway. Over Dad's shoulder were a couple and two kids. I blinked but it was still true. No Mum.

Dad turned around. "Summer! Come and meet our new neighbors."

I tucked myself into his side and couldn't meet their eyes.

"This is my youngest. These are the Witkins from next door. Mike and Julie."

"G'day, Summer. That's a very pretty name." The woman crouched down to speak to me as if I were a kid half my age. She wore a white visor and all-black gym gear. She was tanned and toned with iridescent cheeks like the inside of a shell.

"Um . . . well . . ." I went blank.

"She's not usually this shy," said Dad.

"Probably still jet-lagged." The man lowered himself to say this to me, just like his wife had done. Then he ruffled the top of my hair. "Mind you," he continued, straightening up, "we can barely get a word out of my boy, either, and he hardly goes farther than the end of the street! So what's his excuse? Hahaaa!" He slapped the tall boy beside him on the back and the boy's body gave in to the shove as if he was used to it.

"Mike, cut it out," the woman said through gritted teeth. They were the whitest teeth I'd ever seen. "Summer, this is our son, Milo, and this is our daughter, Sophie. Sophie's nine, aren't you, Soph?"

Sophie nodded and smiled as her mother steered her by the shoulders and parked her right in front of me. Sophie had a few missing teeth and she was holding a doll that looked like it was wearing even more makeup than my sister. It felt like this lady was suggesting that I should be friends with Sophie just because we were the same height. I had to say something, fast.

"I turn thirteen today."

"You're joshing me!" said Mrs. Witkin. "Well, you're only a couple of years younger than Milo here. What a sweet petite thing you are!"

Dad was staring at me, and I knew why. It wasn't because he was thinking, like I was, that this woman was annoying. It was because he'd forgotten what today was: my birthday. Completely and utterly forgotten.

I watched his face as he pictured a mental calendar and realized how stupid he was, by which time mine was hot with shame. I should never have come downstairs.

"We were inviting you all to come round to ours tonight," said Mrs. Witkin. "Just a barbecue, nothing fancy. But now it can be a birthday party! Hey, Summer? What do you think of that?"

I so badly wanted to tell Mrs. Witkin *exactly* what I thought. That where I'd kept every loving feeling I'd once had for my family was now an infected wound. That despite everything, my thirteenth birthday could still slip their minds. I wanted to say, "Mrs. Witkin, naturally I also hate *myself.*" And, "Mrs Witkin, I cannot stand to be around a single human being on this planet, let alone strangers, let alone strangers like you who smile this much."

"Thank you," I said in a puny voice. I tried to nudge Dad's foot so he'd deal with the situation for me. Surely he wasn't going to let this happen, this last-minute, pretend thirteenth-birthday party with complete strangers.

"That's so kind of you," he said. "Me and the girls had better get our acts together. We'll be round at six. What can we bring?"

"Don't you dare bring a thing." Julie playfully tapped my dad's arm. "See you at six!"

So it was actually going to happen. How could he think *this* was what I felt like doing for the birthday he'd forgotten about? How could I have let myself believe that Mum would actually come? Thinking about her was so painful, I had no choice but to block her from my mind for good.

The woman, Julie Witkin, herded her family down our front path and out the gate, then through their own gate and up their path.

"Dad."

"I'm so sorry about your birthday, sweetheart. I'll make it up to you."

"How about by not making me go? I can't think of anything worse."

"It'll be great, Summer. They seem like such nice people. I told you us Aussies were like that!"

"I hate them."

He laughed. He actually laughed at me.

"My sweet, sweet Summer. This isn't like you. Look, I'll get a cake from down the road. Biggest you've seen. And I'll buy you whatever you like." He wrapped his arms around me and lifted me off the ground. I stayed stiff and still. "Where's my Summer, hey? Where's my little girl? Where did she go?"

I was too angry to give him the answer that was forming hard as a weapon inside me. *That* Summer already felt as impossible to reach as Floyd or Mum did, a tiny and deeply buried apple seed. My defenses from now on would be thick as an oven glove, keeping out the warmth of Dad holding me, keeping everything out.

the other side of
a name

The morning after the barbecue from hell, I came downstairs to find Wren and Dad wearing fixed grins and holding cards, as if my birthday could just be shifted to the next day with no consequences. There was also a small parcel on the kitchen bench, covered in airmail stickers. To get here from London, it must have been sent before we'd even left.

"Open it, then," said Dad.

I could see it was Mal's writing. "Maybe later."

"Mum and Gran sent their love."

"When?"

"Skype. You were fast asleep. We tried to wake you." They couldn't have tried that hard. "You'd better switch on your phone so that people can get in touch with you."

I'd turned it off when we left London, and that's how it was going to stay.

Wren's card was a hand-drawn portrait of me. It was brilliant, but I kept my face stony. Dad's card had a huge shiny thirteen on the front, and a hundred-dollar note inside. It was the first time I'd held Australian money, and it felt as fake as everything else here did.

"But wait! That's not all," he said, lifting a huge, long box out from behind the counter. I had already guessed what was inside but I unwrapped it slowly, waiting to feel something like the way opening presents was supposed to feel.

It was a guitar: black, brand-new, and three-quarter sized, for shrimps like me.

"Your first very own guitar," said Dad.

I held it stiffly and tried to smile because in my head I knew he was being thoughtful. But my heart only wanted the Ibanez Artwood.

Later, Dad said, to make my birthday even more special, we were going to pick up the puppy. I swore I wouldn't love that thing either. There wasn't room inside me for anything else but white-hot anger.

———————

Dad honked the horn of the rental car and I trudged slowly down the stairs. Wren was waiting at the bottom, and something about her made me do a double take. Was she dressed differently? No, even in this raging heat she had on her layers of black clothes and her thick makeup. It was her expression. It didn't say "I hate you" anymore.

"What?" she said. But it was a different kind of "what." Curious instead of murderous.

"Nothing." I realized that, since we'd arrived, Wren hadn't said a single mean thing to me. It was wasted, though, because I didn't even have room to feel relief.

The rental car smelled of plastic and lemony boiled sweets.

"What's going to happen to Dorrit?" I said. "We just left her at the airport."

"Harry said he'd pick her up." Harry was Dad's oldest friend. "He's got a double garage so he'll take care of her until . . . Well, he'll take care of her."

I caught Dad's nervous look in the rearview mirror. Nothing more had been said about when Mum might be coming. Because she wasn't.

We arrived at a rundown house with a bare and dusty front garden. The walls of the place were painted wooden planks, but some were broken or missing, and the rest were peeling. One window was boarded up, and the porch was covered in bits of junk. The house sagged on one side like a shipwreck.

"Are you sure you've bought a puppy, Dad?" said Wren. "This place does not say cute baby animals to me. More like dawn raids and multiple arrests."

Dad had gone very quiet. A woman came out, carrying a black puppy and using one of its paws to wave at us. At the same time we heard a deeper bark coming from somewhere nearby.

"There you go. Everything's fine," said Dad.

"Is that one ours?" said Wren.

"No, ours is a golden color. Come on, let's go and see."

We got out of the car and went with Dad. The puppy woman said, "Follow me," with a smile, and Dad made small talk as we were led down the side of the house toward a tall wooden gate.

"She's back here," said the woman.

"She?" said Dad. By then the gate had been opened and before he knew it Dad had a pair of legs over his shoulders. "Oh my God!"

"Down, puppy!" sang the woman.

"Puppy? What sort of puppy do you call this?" said Dad as he tried to angle his mouth away from the dog's baggy tongue. Standing on her back legs, she was as tall as my six-foot dad. She had wiry fur, a long whiskery snout, and a nose like a lump of coal.

"Technically they're puppies until they're two."

"And how old is she?"

"Turns two next week."

Dad was still being ambushed.

"But—But the ad said she was a golden retriever."

The woman addressed the creature in her arms instead of Dad. "Exactly. She's a golden retriever cross, isn't she, Muffin?"

The dog licking Dad's face looked nothing like a golden retriever, except for the light gold fur and *maybe* the eyes. She finally stopped licking Dad and ran past us. She lay on her tummy by the gate, regally, like one of the lions in Trafalgar Square. Then she put her head on one paw in the exact same pose as in the photo we had of when she was tiny.

"Crossed with what?" said Dad.

"A donkey?" said Wren through the corner of her mouth.

"It didn't say cross on the website," said Dad. "I wasn't expecting something so . . ."

"Excuse me, but I think you'll find it did." The woman was still smiling, talking to us in a baby voice as if we were puppies too. But I got the sense she could turn at any moment.

Dad got a piece of paper out of his back pocket: the original printout. "Golden retriever . . . X. Oh.

You mean the X stands for cross?"

"Exactly. And I don't do refunds."

Dad and Wren followed the woman down the path toward the dog. I stayed back. The dog looked up at Dad as he went down on one knee. He stroked her on the top of her scraggly head until she swiveled to make his hand go under her chin instead. Then she started making a low-pitched grunty moan deep inside that made Dad and Wren laugh.

"She loves that," said Wren.

"You hate dogs," I muttered, but I was too far away for them to hear. "Dogs are idiots, remember?"

Dad got down lower still and let the dog lick his face.

Wren looked back at me. "They're tragic. Totally tragic." The corner of her mouth twitched, hinting at a smile. Without thinking it through, I walked over to her side and said, "You got over Charlotte pretty quickly."

Wren looked at me, stunned, as if I'd actually hit her.

"Right. One of you has to name her," said Dad.

"You mean we're actually taking this thing?" said Wren.

"Of course you are," said the woman. "You're lucky to've skipped the chewing phase. This one's a keeper. Walks by your side, crosses the road by herself—doesn't even need a lead. I'll get the papers."

Dad was completely sold on this giant puppy. That was obvious.

"Summer? What do you think we should call her?" said Dad. "Or Wren? Even though I know you're more of a cat person . . ."

I could see that Wren was thinking. She'd have some smarty-pants, obscure name that only made sense to her. I looked desperately around for ideas.

"Come on," said Dad. "What does she remind you of?"

"*I* think . . . I . . . think . . ." I tried to stall. I couldn't let Wren name her. But there was no inspiration in this place. . . . Until, suddenly, a movement caught my eye around the dried-up lavender bush. "Bee."

"Bea? That's lovely! As in Beatrice?" said Dad.

"I suppose."

Dad and Wren were both looking at me.

"I don't care. Call it whatever you want!" I stormed out of the front gate, nearly knocking it off its hinges.

On the way home, the dog took up most of the back seat, even with its head sticking out the window.

———

So the dog was Dad's, and mostly Dad called her "Lady" instead of Bee anyway. She had a kennel in the garden but she could only get the back half of her body into it. You could tell that Dad never made her use it by the enormous dog-shaped patch of coarse hair at the end of Dad's bed.

I kept the promise I'd made to myself. Bee was nothing to do with me. Instead, I had decided that I shouldn't waste the new guitar, so I put in the hours, just like Floyd had when he was my age. My finger-tips built up their calluses again. Eventually, my chord changes became smoother. In a few weeks I'd learned enough chords to play tons of songs. The way a tiny change in a chord could take the music from one mood to another captivated me. Like starting with an A major—index finger on the D string, second fret, middle finger on the G string, second fret, and ring finger on the B string, second fret—and then lifting off my index finger. I found out the tricks for playing with small hands, like strumming more precisely so that I didn't have to put my thumb on the lower E string. There were tricks for having a higher singing voice, too, like using a capo to change the key. I used the hundred-dollar note to buy picks and a tuner.

When I played, it wasn't about feeling or soul, it was just about the notes and being better at playing them than I had been the day before.

the other side of
a Crowd

THREE MONTHS LATER

"Je m'appelle Summer. J'habite à Melbourne. J'ai une sœur et un père et un chien jaune et brun. Elle s'appelle Bee."

"Formidable, Summer! Maintenant, Becky, s'il vous plaît..."

Becky Wong, the girl next to me, took her turn. Only fifteen minutes to go until the last lesson of the last day of the week was over. I scanned the room and calculated that it was safe to zone out, because by the time Madame Dufour had listened to every student, the bell would ring.

I couldn't wait to get out of there. The boxes we'd packed in London all those weeks ago had arrived by ship and been cleared through customs: finally we'd have our old stuff back. I pictured it bursting out of the boxes like party poppers, landing in all the wrong places. I only really wanted one particular thing. Dad said that Gran had promised it had made the container along with all our other stuff. But of course I didn't trust what Gran said anymore. I still hadn't spoken to her—or to Mum—since we'd left.

Becky nudged me to show me a secret thumbs-up inside her stretched-out sweater sleeve. She smiled with clear brown eyes that looked like they never cried. When Madame had sprung the speaking test on us just now, I'd written out the answers for her. Becky was always nervous in this class and often asked for my help. French was the only subject I *could* help her with. It was everything else about this school that seemed like another language.

"Do you want to hang out after?" Becky whispered.

"I can't," I whispered back instinctively. This bit was always awkward with Becky. I'd managed to put most people off, but she was slow to get the message.

"Do you have to help your dad again?"

"Yep. Every Friday."

That was a lie. I didn't spend any time with Dad at all. I think Wren and I were free range again, but it was hard for me to tell because I didn't have anywhere

I wanted to go. Becky was sweet and from the way she spoke about her parents—as though she actually got on with them—I knew she'd still like me if I kept giving that excuse. And I couldn't help wanting Becky to like me. She was funny, always sort of nervous, and full of energy. In another life we'd have been friends, but we were just friend*ly*, and that was different. It was an adjective. "Friend" was a noun, solid and true.

Australia was so much more complicated than it had looked on TV. I was swamped every single day by information that was probably in everyone else's DNA. Everything seemed new, from calling crisps "chips" to how many states and territories there were.

On my first day I wasn't the only one who looked new and terrified. Sameena, who had come from India, started on the same day. We'd had to stand up in class and introduce ourselves.

Sameena had stumbled through her story with bits of English, smiling the whole time. Her parents were studying here, and they would only be in Australia for a year. Then they'd go home. She made that word sound beautiful, with a whispery "h" and a hard "o" and a stretched-out "m." She said she wanted to make the most of being here.

When it was my turn to speak I kept it as bland as possible. "Dad was born here. It seems really nice."

Everyone.

    Seems.

        Really.

            Nice.

The wind had changed, and I was stuck like this. I couldn't be like Sameena, even though I knew deep down that she had it right. We always smiled at each other, but we didn't have a special new-kid bond. Because to me she looked like part of things now. Sometimes I felt ashamed of being this miserable, but still I kept my head down at school and ran back to our house, to my own room, as soon as the bell rang. That feeling would be even stronger after tomorrow when I'd filled the room with my old things. And that one, single, most precious object.

Finally French was over and school was out for another day. We spilled out of every classroom like polystyrene balls escaping out of a beanbag, skittering in all directions. There were over a thousand students here, and I was learning how to fit in on the surface: long hair in a high ponytail, ribbon optional, and a blue-and-white-checked dress worn as short as you could get away with. The boys wore gray shorts and the older ones looked like a strange mix of boy and man, with hairy legs and massive black shoes the same size as Dad's.

I couldn't help picturing Floyd walking down these corridors with me. He'd have found a way to make the uniform cool. People would have followed him. They always did.

The crowd noise grew as we went past the metal lockers. The glass cabinets of sports trophies were next, and then the school photos from years stretching back to the days when Dad was a kid. This was his old school. I think I was supposed to feel some sort of connection because of that, but I didn't.

The school motto was "Kindness, Industry, Knowledge." Here's how I saw it. "Kindness"—saying no *politely* to every invitation. "Industry"—working hard to stay out of everyone's way. "Knowledge"— understanding that I'd never, ever fit in.

Wren fell into step beside me.

"Text from Dad," she said. "We're having dinner next door."

"Again?"

"Guess so."

"No way. I'm not going. Sophie drives me crazy." Wren's elbow delivered an instant dead arm, and I noticed the lanky figure on her other side: Milo, Sophie's big brother. He had an earphone in the ear closest to us and gave me a crooked half smile. I figured he hadn't heard me.

The sea of students washed me closer to the school exit. I couldn't wait to breathe again.

"You don't have to hang out with Soph tonight," said Wren. "Does she, Milo?" Wren really had dialed the sisterly hatred back to almost zero, and held it there.

"Course not. But my mum can be persuasive. . . ."

Milo was awkward, with hair black as a raven's all swept forward onto his pale face. I liked him. He was kind, he spoke softly, and he seemed to live in his own space, like I did. It didn't surprise me: his parents were horrible. I'd overheard them in the garden once, when I'd been sitting in the lemon tree. Mr. Witkin was complaining about something Milo had or hadn't done and then out of the blue he'd said, "Why'd you have to name him after a bloody chocolate drink anyway, Jules?" And she'd whispered back, only it was so loud and low it was more like a growl, "He's not on the spectrum because of his *name*, Michael. Maybe if you were a better father . . ." And from then on I understood that Milo wasn't "normal" enough for his family. Mr. Witkin probably wanted a tough, sporty boy for a son. He'd have loved Floyd. Instead, the Witkins acted like they'd adopted my dad.

"So just hang out with us, Summer," said Wren.

I never thought I'd say this, but I hated the change in her. It felt like another betrayal. At least she was still the same to look at. Still had the most messed-up hair you'd ever see, like someone had dumped a laundry basket of black clothes upside down on her head.

In the middle of my thoughts, my eyes caught on someone who made my heart snag. A woman right down on the other end of the corridor. It was Mum, side-on. It was Mum! She was talking to Mr. Connolly, the principal. Mum! She was here! Why was she here? How did she . . . ? What did she . . . ? It didn't matter. I walked faster, kicking the heel of a girl in front.

"Ow! Careful!" The girl's ponytail caught me in the face as she gave me a dirty look.

I started to say sorry, but the only word in my head was "Mum" and out it came.

"What?" said Wren. "What about Mum?"

I ignored her. Mum was in *my* sights, not hers. I had to get to her first. People's heads were getting in the way. I couldn't get past the crowds.

Then Mr. Connolly turned and walked away and, with her head bowed, Mum walked toward us. I held my breath.

Even after the moment I knew it wasn't her.

Even after I'd rapidly counted every single difference between this woman and my mum.

Even after she'd looked straight into my eyes and away again.

Wrong eyes, longer chin, too pale. Not Mum.

I breathed out, and hoped I'd gotten away with the stupid mistake apart from a funny look from Wren. This wasn't the first time it had happened. I'd seen her many times. Gran and Mal, too. I'd seen kids from my old school, cousins we hadn't visited in years, old teachers, friends of Wren's and Floyd's, the woman from the corner shop. . . . They were flesh-and-blood ghosts. In supermarkets, on the tram, in the background of a news story on television. It hit me the same every time: that heart-soaring moment of possibility—it's really them; *it is!*—followed by reality sinking in like water into sand.

It scared me, how much I'd hoped this woman was Mum. I felt stupid for letting the anger go like a helium balloon. But I grabbed the string again and held it even tighter. People weren't reliable. My own eyes weren't reliable. I just had to hope that the one thing I could depend on, the Ibanez Artwood, would make it to this side of the world.

the other side of
the fence

Saturday morning dragged on as I waited for the van to arrive. Dad went out for an early run with Julie Witkin, which he now did three times a week even though he'd never exercised once in my whole life. It was no wonder he didn't mind spending time with her, the way that woman fussed all over him. He was looking fit and healthy again, but that didn't make it any easier to see them running off down the street, side by side.

After his run, Dad got into his suit and went to work his usual half-day Saturday, showing a bunch of nosy people around houses for sale. I wondered about the family living in our house back home. In my mind I furnished it with our things again—the rug was back in its place, the curtains were hung, all our treasures were on display—and I hated to think of the new people poking around, living our lives.

Wren was on Dad's laptop at the dining room table. "Another parcel came for you, by the way," she said. There was a small brown pillow-shaped package on the kitchen bench.

"Uh-huh."

"Aren't you going to open it?"

"Later."

This brought the number up to three. Three unopened parcels from Mal, stuffed into my bottom drawer like secrets.

"How is she?"

"Who?"

"Mal, you dork." She laughed. "Who else?"

"She's fine. Like you care, anyway."

Wren stopped typing for a moment, then started up again. "Stop pacing, Summer. The van'll be here when it's here."

"You can't stop me from walking in my own house. Anyway, what are you doing, writing a book?" I said sarcastically.

"It's an email." She paused, as if she'd forgotten which words to use. "To Mum, actually."

My stomach dropped. "Since when do you do that?"

"Since about the whole time we've been here." Wren sighed and typed another sentence. "You're the only one who doesn't, Summer." Another sentence. And another.

I stared at the back of the laptop, wondering at Wren's words to Mum and Mum's back to her. I knew Dad and Wren had been Skyping Mum and Gran, but I thought that'd be just "What are you doing?" and "What's the weather like?" I'd left the room every time and no one had ever tried to force me back in. (And what did that say?)

"I don't get you, Wren. When did you become so *nice*? Mum didn't want us. Have you forgotten already?"

Wren gave me a sour look but it quickly melted. "She does love us."

"If you say so." I swallowed a lump in my throat and walked out of the room, straight out of the front door and onto our porch.

I hadn't cried in ages. Now that I was, it felt disappointing, like tripping after being so careful. There's nothing new to cry about, I told myself, but I still couldn't stop.

The warmth of the sun on my face made me feel even sillier and more alone. Everything that was beautiful out here, like the multi-colored autumn leaves that had landed in the front garden or drifted onto the porch, made my feelings ugly. My tears flowed freely, as if crying was just a basic, disgusting bodily function that would happen whether I wanted it to or not.

I tried to breathe deeply and wait for it to pass.

Lots of people had benches on their front porches here but I'd never seen anyone sitting on one. The dog was sprawled on ours now. I sat down in the tiny space left beside her. Stupid, giant creature.

Moments later she licked the side of my hand twice. I ignored her. She licked me in the same spot again and when I took my hand away she snuggled in closer and lay her head in my lap. Her ears twitched. I went to push her off but she whined very quietly. So I put my hand lightly on top of her head. Straightaway Bee shifted so that my hand was now under her chin. I scratched her there and she closed her eyes and made such a funny grunting noise that I laughed out loud. She looked at me with only one eye as if to say *keep scratching*. She was leading me, teaching me her language. Finally she put her head down on my lap again and both of her big brown eyes flicked up to meet mine. Then I saw the wisest, most wonderful creature in the world. Bee. How had I ignored her for so long? I felt like the worst human being ever. I'd barely looked at her in three months, and yet here she was offering me love. This beautiful dog that I'd wanted so much.

Maybe it would be okay to let myself love her back a little bit. I bent over and pushed my nose into the warm fur on the back of her neck.

"Bee," I whispered. "Hello."

———————

Later I was in the front garden teaching Bee tricks. She was a fast learner if I showed her first, which is why we were both lying on our backs in the sunshine when the van finally arrived. I sat up and crossed my legs, too nervous to face this moment: Would the Ibanez Artwood be missing, or damaged, or could I dare to hope? Bee sat right behind me, and my head rested against the warm fur on her chest. We watched Dad direct the boxes inside.

The last object the delivery man carried out of the van was fat with bubble wrap. I got up and a second later, so did Bee.

"That one's for me," I said to the man.

"Can you manage it?" he said, handing it over.

"Of course I can," I snapped. "Sorry, I mean, thank you."

It took ages to unwrap because I couldn't use scissors or a knife just in case. When Wren held up two chipped mugs she'd unpacked, I got even more worried. But finally it was out, and it was as perfect as the last time

I saw it. I suppose that if you can survive a bomb, you can survive anything. A tiny part of me softened toward Gran for making sure it got here.

Wren and Dad stayed inside the house sorting through the boxes. They were getting excited about where to put everything. I didn't want to watch them try to slot our old life into our new one. I had what I needed.

The porch bench was my new favorite spot and Bee agreed. She sat right beside me, which was just as well because the guitar was still too big for me, and I needed to rest my arm on her back to hold it comfortably.

—*I hope you're going to play this time, Summer.*

Floyd was back. I felt scared and excited, and somehow shy. *I've been waiting and waiting, Floyd. I missed you so much.*

—*I'm here now. Come on, play.*

But Milo was in his front yard shooting hoops. I wasn't ready to play my brother's guitar in front of other people. For now I was happy getting used to the feel of it again. So I sat on the bench with Bee and the guitar, watching Milo. In between missing his shots, Milo started to shoot me a question or a comment over the low fence.

"Must be good to have your stuff back."

"It's the best."

Milo bounced the ball and tried to run but tripped over and landed heavily on his side.

"Ouch. Are you okay, Milo?"

"No damage." He got up, laughed goofily, and started bouncing and shooting again. Or trying to. He had the right clothes for basketball—bright blue and shiny—and I could tell he was concentrating to get his moves right because when he'd go to take a shot his tongue would poke out and he'd frown. But his arms and legs were long and loose like a little kid's drawing, and his feet moved as if his shoes were filled with sand. Out of the last ten balls he'd only gotten one in.

—*Who's he?*

Just one of Wren's friends.

—*Wren and this guy? Wow, I'd never have guessed.*

Not like that.

—*You sure?*

Milo's next shot hit the roof of his house. He flinched and shook his head.

"Do you even *like* basketball?" I said.

"I hate it, but I hate Dad going off at me even more." He sent a worried glance toward his house.

"You should just tell him."

"Yeah? Maybe. It's easier to go along with a few things. I have my own stuff."

"Like what?" I pictured him in a dark room playing a complex strategy game on his computer. He had that look about him.

"I draw."

Oh. I'd read him the wrong way. Drawing was the thing he and Wren had in common. That and the fact that they were both really clever. In the past Wren had always used her brain just to score points. Part of me was tempted to tell Milo what she was really like. It didn't seem fair that she'd reinvented herself.

"What do you draw?"

"Landscapes . . . people . . . I go to the creek with a sketch pad quite a lot. I can think better there. You should check it out, Summer."

His tone made it seem like more than just a throwaway thing to say. "What do you mean, *I* should?"

"Sorry?"

"Why should *I* check out this creek?"

"Don't worry about it, Summer. You don't have to. I just thought . . . I was just trying to be . . . Because you seem . . ."

"What?" I snapped. "What do I seem?" It felt like things had been decided about me and what I was like. I didn't even know what a creek *was*.

"Hey, doesn't matter," and he started his awkward bouncing again.

I knew I was being horrible but I couldn't stop. "Tell me. You started this."

Milo put the ball under his arm. "The creek is a special place. Kind of spiritual. It always helps me when I'm feeling . . . the way we feel sometimes." He used his hand to indicate 'we,' as in him and me.

"What's the way 'we' feel?"

He rested the ball on the fence. "Like we don't belong here. You know, like we landed in the wrong life."

His words were uncomfortably close. "Is that what you feel like, then?"

"Sometimes." He looked back at his house and then at my feet as if the next bit was too much to say to my face. "I have to keep what I'm good at a secret. Because I know they're looking for it, and it's driving them mad not finding it."

I got it. If Milo's parents knew how smart and talented he was, they'd make a huge deal out of it. They paraded Sophie around like a show dog.

"The creek's far away from everything that makes the wrong kind of noise. It's just you, some trees, rocks, water. If the wind's on your side you can't even hear the freeway. It's like being nowhere, in a good way."

"What would I do there? Just sit? I don't draw like you. I'd feel like an idiot."

He shrugged. "Take Floyd's guitar. Play it to nobody."

My eyes stung when he said my brother's name.

"Wren said the guitar means a lot to you."

I'd never imagined that Wren would talk about me.

"Wren hates it when I play," I said, halfheartedly because she'd never once complained about it in Australia, though she'd done it plenty of times back home.

Milo did his usual gangly shrug with joints made of string. "She definitely didn't say *that*." He bounced the ball again, went for a shot, and missed.

At that moment, our door opened and Wren appeared on the porch. She smiled crookedly at Milo as if she'd forgotten how. He did the goofiest salute you could ever imagine, and I felt something completely unexpected: jealousy.

"This must be for you," Wren said, passing me some sheet music stapled in one corner, with a message at the top.

I tried to take it but she wouldn't let go. "Give it!" I snapped.

"Say thank you, then." She gave me surrender hands and an eye roll, then waved to Milo and went back inside.

Without another word, Milo picked up the ball and disappeared through his front door.

The sheets were photocopied ones, and there was some handwriting along the top that hadn't quite come out but was obviously Floyd's. He always wrote in capitals because, like Dad, his handwriting was just scribble.

"THESE ARE FOR YOU. LEARN THEM IN ORDER. WE'LL PLAY THEM TOGETHER ONE DAY."

I swallowed hard and read them again. The first song was "Let It Be" by The Beatles. I could remember being really young and watching Floyd sit on the coffee table performing this one for the whole family for the first time. Dad had been so proud because he'd been the one who'd told Floyd about The Beatles.

Why didn't we find these earlier, Floyd? Where were they? When did you plan on giving them to me?

—I can't answer everything. Does it matter, now that you have them?

Yes . . . No . . . I don't know.

My mind was swimming as I flipped through the pages. There were five songs to learn.

You wanted me to come busking with you. We would have done that together, wouldn't we? Wouldn't we, *Floyd?*

I jumped when Milo came back out of his house. For a second I thought I might have been talking out loud. But he didn't say anything. Instead, from over the fence he held out a map he'd drawn for me. I couldn't believe that's what he'd gone inside to do.

"Here. So you can get to the creek," he said, and he left again without giving me a chance to say "sorry" and "thank you."

The map looked like something out of a fantasy book, with detail and shading and tiny old-fashioned handwriting like I'd seen in Wren's copy of *The Hobbit*. I looked from the map to the songs and shivered, as if a message had bypassed my brain and gone straight to my nerves.

the other side of
a Song

Floyd would often skate all morning and then busk all afternoon at a place called Southbank, by the River Thames. I'd never been. Being older he was allowed to go on bigger adventures, or maybe it was just that Mum and Dad knew they couldn't stop him. I'd always watch him leave. I could picture him now, winding down the road on his board without once faltering over the tarmac lumps and buckled paving stones of our neighborhood streets. The guitar would be against his back like it was as much a part of him as his arms and legs.

And it was that picture that got me up the next morning with my own adventure in mind. I liked to think that he'd be following behind me this time.

—Where are we going?

Just wait and see.

I was still getting used to hearing Floyd in my head again. It made me nervous but excited. Nervous because of the quiet time in between. Excited because I wouldn't be going to the creek alone.

Dad and Wren were still sleeping. "Gone for a walk," I wrote on the back of a supermarket receipt on the kitchen bench. Then I screwed it up, threw it in the bin, and wrote "Gone to buy milk" on the back of one of Dad's flyers, because that was more specific and I hadn't tested out my free-range theory since we'd arrived. I didn't need the weight of Dad's worry on my back as well as the guitar.

I tried to wear the Ibanez Artwood like Floyd used to, but it was so big that it knocked against the backs of my legs as I made my way to the front door. I had Milo's map in my hand and the first of Floyd's songs folded in my pocket.

I passed my own guitar on the way out, propped in a corner. The way I felt about the two instruments was so different. Only one of these objects had a soul.

Once I was out the front, I could smell the morning: tangy cut grass. It was blue-sky pretty, with a chill in the air. The trees were barely clinging to their crispy leaves.

Sophie was out there. She had Rollerblades on, knee pads, elbow pads, and a sparkly purple helmet. *And* she was sitting on a bike.

—Who's this?

Some annoying kid. Ignore her.

"Hi, Summer! Come and play!"

"That's a lot of wheels," I said flatly.

"Mum wants me to be good at both."

"Right."

"I know! I'll rollerblade and you can have a go on my bike!"

The idea of hanging out with Sophie was out of the question, but transport to the creek seemed like a stroke of genius, even if the bike was pink with a heart-shaped bell. I just needed to make the two things separate: yes to bike, no to Sophie.

"How about I take it for a test-drive around the block first?"

"Mum says I'm only allowed to the end of the street and back."

"But I'm older, Soph. I can go farther. You wouldn't mind, would you?"

"What will I get if I say yes?"

"Depends. What do you want?"

"To see your room. And to hang out with you." Her smile dropped and her eyebrows drew together. "*All day.*"

—Wow, this kid is determined! She likes you, sis.

She's only nine. We're not friends. I can't stand her.

—Whoa, Summer . . .

"Fine. It's a deal. Tomorrow after school." I'd find a way to get out of it later. Floyd had no idea what he was talking about. He'd only just got here, after all.

"That's a start, I suppose." I got the feeling that Sophie's main talent wasn't rollerblading but getting her own way. She clambered off her bike awkwardly and held onto the fence while I wheeled it toward me. It was the perfect height for me, which was embarrassing.

"You go off and rollerblade, Soph."

"But you're coming straight back, right? You promised, Summer."

I definitely hadn't. I started pedaling. "Sure. Bye, Soph!"

I got a glimpse of her doubtful eyes as she clung to the fence with both hands. "Okay! Bye, Summer!"

I pedaled away from her down the wide pavement and grinned as I picked up speed. There were young trees on my right and driveways on my left. I rang the heart-shaped bell and was surprised to find that my own heart seemed to ring with a happy feeling. It didn't matter so much about riding a bike that was much too young for me, because no one really knew me here.

The thought made me feel lighter and made me pedal even faster. I could be strange here. I could be different. There was no one to care.

At first it was awkward to ride along with such a big guitar on my back, but once I started I wasn't going back. It was so much quieter here than back home in London, hardly any traffic. I held the map down on the handlebars with my thumbs and stopped at every corner to figure out where to go next.

At the third corner I heard a deep bark. I turned and saw Bee. She'd caught up with me! She raced toward me in a ghostly streak and when she got next to the bike her front legs stopped before her back ones and she almost fell over. I loved the way she was ladylike one minute and lumpish the next.

"Good girl! Coming with me?"

For a moment she sat still with her head on the side, looking at me. Maybe she was wondering if this was a good idea. Or maybe it was her way of telling me off for not taking her with me in the first place.

"Sorry, Bee. I'm used to being by myself, that's all."

She barked once and raced ahead. We were off! She was easily as fast as I was, even with a good wind pushing me from behind. Bee was bigger than the bike, the guitar was nearly bigger than me, and I couldn't help laughing at what we must have looked like.

I felt a rush as I cruised off the pavement and onto the smooth surface of the road, laughing with a ripple in my heart, the way I used to when Floyd would chase me up the stairs.

—*You used to scream your head off.*

I'll scream right now if you like!

—*Go on!*

"Aieeeeeeeee!" I laughed again.

The wind had whipped up the dry leaves from the ground, making them look like they'd decided to come along with us for the ride. A few leaves skimmed the guitar and sailed over my head. Bee jumped up mid-run to snap at them. I barked a laugh and she echoed me happily. On we went, creating a storm of whizzing wheels, racing paws, and flying leaves: a strange sort of crew on some kind of adventure.

———

We were there in ten minutes; Milo's map was perfect. I stopped to look at the entrance sign to this bit of bushland. It had a whole list of warnings about the water as well as some drawings of wildlife to look out for: kookaburras, lorikeets, magpies, frogs, eels, and flying foxes. There was a word hand-painted: Wominjeka. In small letters underneath, the sign said it meant "Welcome" in the language of the Aboriginal people who'd lived here first. I liked that. It felt like I was arriving somewhere special. Bee barked once to hurry me up.

There was a bike path all along the river that stretched around a bend in either direction. I followed Milo's arrows. "Stop here for Growling Grass Frogs (endangered)," the map said. It was amazing: one minute I couldn't hear a thing, the next it was as if the frogs had all started croaking just for me. I stopped the bike for a moment to listen. It was a funny griping sound, as if they were complaining about the weather.

I continued along the path. Sometimes the water sounded like whispering, other times like people clapping. Sometimes it looked deep and dark and other times rocks peeped out and the water frothed around them. I couldn't identify a single plant or tree except for plain old "grass"—and even the grass was a different, tougher kind. Wren's giant paint box didn't have this many greens and browns. I never knew a place could be this lovely without all the other colors.

Milo's biggest cross was on a little rock that looked like it was a short distance from the path, right down the steep slope. As I came close to where I thought it would be, I got off Sophie's bike and wheeled it along. When I was sure I was in the right place, I hid the bike in a bush and headed down, Bee bounding in circles around me with every step I took. Her energy had infected me but I was tired out now. My back was hot and sweaty under my sweater, and I couldn't wait to off-load the guitar and sit down for a rest.

"Look, Bee, that's it there." It was exactly as Milo had drawn it: a flat rock jutting out of the water like a natural dock. Three brown ducks sailed around its edges like small boats. The rock was in the shade of tall trees that crowded the edge of the water, and the mossy ground around it was soft and lumpy like a cushion. I took off the guitar and sat down. Bee's leathery pink tongue was lolling out of the side of her mouth and her ears moved to the sound of birds messaging each other high above us.

The river was murky and tanned, whipped up like someone blowing hard on a cup of tea. Only, this water must have been freezing. I breathed in slowly and tasted leaf and earth, water and sunshine, cold air and silence—all of that. There were silvery needles of light where the sun caught the water as it coursed over tree roots and rocks. It was a place where you could be small and still, just noticing things.

My breath and Bee's breath and the rush of the water were becoming one peaceful sound. Just like Milo had said, it was a place that felt like nowhere else.

Bee caught my eye.

"Like it here?"

She tipped her head to the side as if to say, "Who wouldn't?"

"Me too."

I held the guitar in my lap and pinned down the "Let It Be" sheet music in front of me with a small rock.

"No one will hear me, Bee." Except Floyd, I thought. And hoped.

Bee lay on her belly and rested her head on her front paw.

—*I've waited months for this, Summer.*

I don't want you to be disappointed.

—*As if, Sum.*

I gulped and looked at the chords. There were only four to get right, and a melody for the last line of the verse. Then I began. I was cautious at first, bracing myself for the sting of the steel strings of the Ibanez Artwood, which were harder on the tips of my fingers than the nylon strings of my own guitar. The first chord change was horrible, but I kept going. I pressed a little harder and ran my right thumb down and up. Back up, down again, bolder this time. I was mumbling the words of the chorus, humming the rest, and concentrating on the chords.

Am I doing this right, Floyd?

He didn't answer. Maybe that was his way of pushing me to be better. I was starting to feel the old magic of the two of us playing together. When I closed my eyes I imagined I could hear Floyd's first guitar—the one he used to let me practice on—playing along with me. Soon a joyful laugh was rising in me like bubbles. I carried on, louder and faster and louder and faster.

Suddenly Bee scrambled up on her long legs and barked.

"Sh, it's okay. I'm just practicing." I giggled, feeling silly for getting carried away and spooking my dog. But Bee wouldn't settle. Towering over me, she put her nose in the air and barked again. Come on, Bee, I thought. I didn't ruin the song *that* much.

I plucked out some more notes and tried to make the melody flow more smoothly from my fingers. "Your lessons with me must have stuck, don't you think, Floyd?" I'd never talked to my brother out loud before but it seemed all right in front of our dog and out here. "It's sad you didn't know him, Bee. You two would have got along like a—"

Bee sat down very deliberately and howled. It was sad and insistent and directed across the water to the bank on the other side of the creek.

Over there, a twig snapped. I looked away from Bee and saw a boy stumbling backward and landing awkwardly. There was someone else here? But that side of the river was rough and tangled with trees and shrubs. There was no path over there that I could see.

The boy seemed confused. Shocked, even—I could tell from his movements. I watched as he stared up at the canopy of trees. He looked along the creek each way and then behind him into the brambles and long grass.

I was frightened.

Bee and I stood up together, and I put my hand on her back. This boy looked like he was in trouble. Maybe he was hiding from someone. I had a horrible feeling that I'd stumbled into someone else's drama and should get out of there as quickly as possible.

As I struggled to get off the rock I could hear the boy muttering quite clearly, even though he was over the other side.

"What the . . . ? Holy . . . I must be dreaming. Please let me be dreaming."

I tried to stop staring at him. My fingers fumbled with the guitar strap as I struggled to get it on my back. Bee was dancing on her toes. She looked from me to the boy, me to the boy. As I started to get away, she sat down stubbornly and made a strange whining noise.

"Come on, Bee!" I whispered.

In her eyes I saw longing and sadness. Or did I? That was silly. What did I know about dogs? And what did dogs know about a situation like this? I was in charge here. I had to make a decision, and that was to leave. Dad and Wren didn't even know I was here—no one on Earth did.

But I couldn't help myself; I looked over again. The boy had stepped out of the trees' shade and onto a rock that was in direct sunlight. Now I saw him properly, and a sound halfway between a gasp and a cry came out of my mouth as it hit me: I'd seen that face before.

the other side of
the creek

"Who are you?" said the boy across the water. But that was *my* question. "What is this place?" He looked more terrified than I was, as if he honestly had no idea where we were.

"It's called Wurun Creek." I felt for Milo's map but decided not to show the boy I had one. The uncertainty of being new around here suddenly hit me. "It's only a minute from the road on this side. I don't know it very well. I'm from . . . somewhere else . . ."

At first I thought he hadn't heard me, but then he looked right at me again. "I've heard of it. But I don't think I've ever been here before." He sat down on the rock and put his head in his hands.

This spooked feeling I had reminded me of all the times I'd seen the spitting images of Mum and Gran and Mal since we'd been here, and that pocket of time in which I'd truly believe it was them. Why did this boy at the creek make me feel that way? If I had seen him before, he'd just be someone I'd seen on a tram, at school, or in the supermarket. I'd seen a thousand new faces since we'd arrived.

My brain still said run. But adrenaline had drained down my legs and into the rock I was standing on, gluing my feet to it like stubborn snails. My heart was pounding. Bee lay down on her belly, panting happily. Some guard dog she turned out to be.

"Do you go to Fairfield High?" I said.

The boy was still looking down when he muttered an answer, so I didn't hear it.

"What did you say?"

He looked up as if he'd forgotten I was there. "I said no. Is this a dream?"

"Um, n-no?"

He looked around again and started swearing under his breath. Then he got onto his knees and crawled to the edge of the rock. He looked as if he was going to scoop up some water, but instead he just stared at his hand.

"Be careful," I said, surprising myself. "It could be deep."

I couldn't explain why I was worried about him. It was stupid. I got up again. What was I even doing here? Dad would blow a fuse if he could see me. "Come on, Bee."

"Wait! Please! Don't go."

He looked so scared again. But what did he think *I* could do about it? My brain kept winding back through memories to find where his face fit in. Train station, swimming pool, the line for the cinema . . .

"This *is* a dream, isn't it?" he said.

"What are you talking about?"

"I'm lost. I don't know. . . ." He bent over and rested his hands on his knees. "I don't know where I am."

"I can't help you. I'm sorry. I only know how to get back to the main road from this side."

I had to stop talking. This boy might be crazy. Otherwise why would he think he was dreaming? He could be on drugs. Look at him, I told myself, he has wild dreadlocks and his clothes are shabby and . . . I stopped that thought, angry with myself for sounding like an adult full of prejudices. It didn't matter how this boy was dressed. The reason I needed to leave was that he was a stranger acting strangely.

"What's your name?" he said.

I panicked. "Sophie."

"Where are you from? You sound different."

"London."

He sat down and started shivering. "Why is it so cold here?"

I couldn't feel the cold at all. "I'm going," I said. "My dad's waiting for me up this path."

"No! I don't know how I got here. I know how strange that sounds, but I was asleep. I think." He held his head again. "I don't remember. Then suddenly here I am. It doesn't make sense."

I turned. "I can't help you!" I shouted back. At first my feet seemed to stick, but then a sudden rush of air hit me from behind, and I found I could run as fast as I wanted. I looked back once but couldn't see him. Was he hiding? Would he jump out at me someplace else? I ran clumsily up the side of the bank. The brambles tore lines into my skin as I pulled out Sophie's bike.

The fear went deeper than seeing a stranger across a river. It felt like my heart would never slow down.

the other side of
Bee

The journey back to the house had none of the fizz of the journey to the creek. I wasn't an adventurer after all. Bee ran alongside me. When she looked at me her eyes seemed reproachful, but I didn't really trust what I was seeing. She barked once and it unnerved me; I almost fell off the bike. Then I felt betrayed. I'd finally let her in but she hadn't been on my side back there.

I noticed different things on the journey this time. The way the trees held out their bare arms like old wicker chairs left out in bad weather. They looked helpless, like they'd been unraveling slowly. Unraveling was what could happen to me if I wasn't more careful.

I made a fresh promise to stay coiled up tight, not to go out, and not to let anyone in.

Floyd? Are you there?

—Always. You know that.

But you weren't with me back at the creek, were you? You didn't see the boy?

—Calm down, Summer. Just get home.

Finally the roads became familiar, and then I hit Lime Street. "*Sensationally positioned! The family home of your dreams.*" That boy had thought he was in a dream. . . .

A pair of pink Rollerblades lay abandoned on the pavement, but a moving object caught my eye: a grasshopper girl bouncing on a giant trampoline enclosed in high mesh walls.

"There you are!" Sophie whined through her cage. "You were *aaages!*" She stopped bouncing and pressed her face into the mesh like a tiny bank robber.

I propped her bike against the fence.

"You stole my bike, Summer. You went really far. I timed you—you were thirty minutes and forty-six seconds exactly. I'm telling."

It was hard not to snap at her, but I had to keep her on my side. "But you're coming over to my house tomorrow, aren't you, Sophie?" I wished I'd given the boy anyone's name but hers. Not that it mattered now.

"If you tell on me, Soph, I'll be grounded and I won't be allowed to have friends over."

"Am I your friend now?"

"If you keep my secret safe you are."

"Deal!" She went to the middle of the trampoline and became a happy grasshopper again—star jump, spin, backward flip—shouting "Secrets! Secrets! Secrets!" with every bounce. "Watch me, Summer!"

"Very good, Sophie." I gave her my best fake smile but my mouth felt crimpled inside like a snail wrenched off the ground. I watched her for a few more seconds to sweeten her promise not to tell. But hating her was becoming like a bitter medicine, and the feeling that she didn't truly deserve it made the dose stronger.

Once I'd escaped and made it back inside our house, I took the guitar off. The back of it had all my warmth while my own skin was cold and clammy. It was as if the guitar were alive while I had turned into a bloodless thing.

I went straight to the kitchen sink and stuck one side of my face underneath cold running water. The feeling that the boy was familiar wouldn't go away. I switched sides, letting the cold water run into the corner of my mouth and gulping hard. The thought of him went straight to my heart and made me too aware of its beating, like when I thought of my brother.

"You're back," said Wren, walking in. "Where's the milk?"

I went straight past her as if she didn't exist, and ran up the stairs.

It was a surprise to find Bee in my room. She was already stretched out and snoozing. I wondered what Dad would think, now that Bee had switched sides and become mine.

"I wish you could talk, Bee." Because it struck me what Sophie had said back there: that I'd been thirty minutes. Thirty minutes? That was impossible. It was ten minutes there and ten minutes back just from our house to the sign that said "Wominjeka." Then there was finding the rock, practicing the four chords, and that conversation with the boy.

I reminded myself that she was only nine years old. She probably couldn't even tell the time.

the other side of losing things

That night, sleep covered every part of me like an over-sized blanket. It was strange because usually sleep was like a too-small blanket and my feet would poke out of the end and get cold or the sleep would fall off me completely and I'd wake in the dark. There was nothing as lonely as being awake in the night when no one else was.

The next morning I woke slowly and peacefully. Still with my eyes closed, I stretched out and flexed every muscle. An orange sherbet light had snuck under my window blinds and settled in my eyelashes. I could feel that it was very early. The melody from "Let It Be" was caught up in a breeze somewhere in the back of my mind.

Suddenly my eyes snapped open. Floyd's music: I'd left it at the creek, abandoned it on that rock like a piece of rubbish.

—*You'll remember the chords, Summer. It's okay.*

No! No! It's not okay! It's a piece of you.

I checked the time. School wasn't for another two hours; I could make it.

I couldn't get dressed fast enough. I ran down the stairs and through the house in my socks, Bee's paws tapping against the floorboards behind me. I opened the front door and put my shoes on standing on one leg on our prickly welcome mat. Bee ran out, peed on the grass, then turned around to show that she was waiting for me. It was as if she knew exactly where we were going.

Sophie's bike was in the same place I'd propped it the day before. Things were left outside much more here than in London. Here they trusted people not to steal bicycles, scooters, and all sorts of things. Dad was always going on to the neighbors about how great that was. Then a conversation would start up that turned London into something out of a Charles Dickens book: dark backstreets teeming with robbers. I hated it when Dad did that. Maybe that was why I decided I'd take the bike without asking.

"Ready?" I whispered.

Bee wagged her tail.

"Good girl. Let's go."

This time I didn't need Milo's map. Bee remembered the way. It was colder today, though; the sherbet light had been a tease and now the sky was flat gray. The wind had a vicious whistle in it but wet leaves stuck stubbornly to the ground. If it had rained all night, what would that have done to my music sheet?

We found the bush with the bike-shaped hole and I shoved Sophie's bike into it. I scrambled down the slope to the rock but I could already see that the paper wasn't where I'd left it. The stone I'd used as a paperweight had stayed put but now all it was pinning down was a pulpy white corner. I scanned the area for the rest of it. The creek tumbled relentlessly past with the leaves and sticks that had fallen from the trees and the junk tossed in along the way.

"It's not here, Bee," I said. "It's lost." The volume of the river was twice as loud.

Bee went to the water's edge, wagging her tail as she looked across to the other side.

I stormed back up the bank and grabbed the bike roughly, feeling so angry with myself for not taking better care of something Floyd had given me.

I was relieved when Bee caught up with me and looked at me in a way I was starting to rely on.

School was even worse than usual that day. The noises were louder and the hundreds of bodies towering over me were even higher. I felt farther away and like I understood even less about this place than when I first got here. Loneliness had shrunk me to a painful dot. My head was throbbing and I couldn't concentrate.

Becky noticed, of course. During math in the afternoon she walked up to Ms. Kumar and talked quietly to her while looking in my direction.

"Becky will take you to the nurse, Summer," Ms. Kumar said kindly.

But I'm not really sick, I thought. And I don't want anyone's kindness, like gentle fingers trying to tear into my hard skin, trying to open me up.

Becky's hand touched my back as we walked out of the classroom. I walked faster to make her touch go away and only shrugged when she tried to talk to me.

The nurse checked my temperature, looked at my tongue, and asked me if I'd eaten that day.

"I think I'm just homesick," I said.

"That's not really a sickness, Summer." She said it so gently I wanted to scream.

Part of me wanted to tell someone about the creek, the lost music sheet, and the strange boy, but what could anyone do with that information except laugh at me? The nurse said I was to go along to my next class after drinking the cup of tea she'd made me. I looked at it. It was pale beige like ladies' tights and lukewarm like most of the ways people tried to make you feel better when they didn't have a clue what was wrong with you.

At the end of the day, on my way out of school, I thought I heard Becky calling my name, but I didn't turn around.

the other side of
midnight

It was warm that night, not like any autumn we were used to. Dad insisted on asking the Witkins over for a barbecue in our garden instead of theirs for a change, so Sophie would have got her way whether or not I'd made the bargain with her.

I had to watch Julie Witkin bustle around our kitchen, opening our drawers and fridge, pointing out all the things we needed. "You seem to be out of extra virgin." "Don't you have a grater, Dougie? I'll get you one like mine." If Mum had been here, and if she had drunk more than two glasses of wine, her barbed words would have flown out and stuck in Julie Witkin's buttercream face.

But she wasn't.

And then there was Sophie to deal with.

"Let's go to your room." She was trying to be cute and conspiratorial, with her shoulders bunched up to her ears and her hands cupped around her mouth.

"Can't. I've got homework."

"But you said. And if you *don't*, I might have to tell the *seeeecret*."

"Sh! All right, but not in my room. Come outside."

So I had to spend the rest of the evening making crowns for her out of leaves and flowers. Sophie was as happy as a ladybird, no matter how much I scowled at her. The whole time she gabbled on, I looked up at my bedroom window, wanting to be holding the Ibanez Artwood and learning the next piece, wanting it to be just me and Floyd.

I played the melody from "If I Were a Boy" in my head while we sat around eating Dad's burned chicken kebabs and Julie's weird salad.

———

Finally they were gone. Dad and Wren had washed up and gone to bed, and the house was quiet. I got out of bed and stood with the Ibanez Artwood by the open window.

The room was stuffy and the night air was wafting

in the scent of tight early blossoms on the lemon tree. I stuck the second song sheet to the window frame, so it was lit by the huge dinner-plate moon.

E minor to C ninth to G to Dsus . . . I was fixed on the dots Floyd had drawn, each one representing a fingertip, and had to concentrate to stop my brain from moving faster through the song than I could change chords. But I was making music. I sang the lyrics, soft as a cat's purr.

Suddenly I noticed movement out of the corner of my eye and stopped playing. Down in the garden. A cat? Or a possum? No, I could see better now—it was much, much bigger. Under the tree, crouching. My hand was frozen in E minor. It was a some*one*. Not Dad or Wren—the someone had longer legs and was wearing a hood.

I ducked out of sight, and pulled the guitar strap over my head so I could lay it down gently. Slowly I rose just enough to take another look. He was still there, standing at full height now. He had sharp, wild animal movements, his hands out for balance even though his feet were planted on solid ground. I sank back down and tried to think what to do. There wasn't a single sound except for the ones I was making.

I peered above the bottom of the window frame again, and this time I saw Bee. She was out there with him! She was sniffing at his legs. What was she doing outside? What if that hooded man wanted to hurt Bee, or take her away? I started to panic. It was my fault; I'd forgotten to call her in for the night.

No one was going to take my beautiful dog. I ran down the stairs and across the cool wooden floors to the locked French doors, slid them open, and prepared to scream my head off.

But he'd gone. There was no sign of him. Nothing to see, and no sounds of footsteps or someone scrambling over the fence. I looked everywhere, dizzily, and now I could hear animal noises: some brushtail possums hissing and coughing. Then a cat landed heavily in the flower bed. I started to doubt everything I'd seen. Bee trotted over and nuzzled my hand with her wet nose. She didn't look scared, or like she'd been guarding us and needed praising. But surely, even in the wide, dark night, I wasn't imagining this sense of something newly gone.

Floyd?

—What is it? Are you scared?

I'm okay now you're here.

A sudden wind swept over me like a lick of cold paint and I wrapped my arms around myself.

I brought Bee in and we went back upstairs. Bee lay down on the landing, stretching out between my room and Wren's. She nearly reached the whole way.

I was suddenly tired. I got into bed but just as I closed my eyes I realized what was missing. I leaped up and grabbed at the Blu-Tack on the window frame that had held the music sheet in place. Shoving half my body out of the window, I scanned the lawn and the bushes and sought out the dark corners, but there was no precious white paper there. I was too scared to go back out and look for it properly. Autumn leaves were being carried high up and far over the surrounding fences by a wind with new strength. I pictured Floyd's music landing in some stranger's backyard. I pictured the neighbor puzzling over the paper for a moment and then screwing it up for the bin. . . . No, that was too hard. I pictured it again, flying and flying like a bird but never landing.

I lay back in bed again and cried a little. I was getting everything so wrong. Why hadn't I shouted for Wren or Dad the way anyone normal would have if they'd seen someone in the backyard who shouldn't have been there? What was happening to me?

I reached over to the Ibanez Artwood on the floor beside me and tugged the E hard between my forefinger and thumb. Buried under the echo of the note there was a shift in the room. I froze, my hand hovering over the strings as the soft vibration came to an end.

153

Floyd? Is it you?

He didn't answer.

Are you there, Floyd? Speak to me!

I could hear something. No, it was different to hearing. Deeper. Someone in here, sharing this space. I wanted to look around the room, but I was terrified. I squeezed my eyes shut. Waited. Very slowly I pulled my cold hand back under the covers. I tried to move farther down so that my head was almost covered. Then I just stayed there, feeling as though every clock had stopped ticking, my shallow breaths growing warmer.

the other side of
Suspicion

In the morning my first thought was that I was
definitely alone. I wasted no time scrambling off
the bed and locking my bedroom door. The sense
of an intruder was still strong, even though it was
an impossible thing to have happened. It surprised
me that sleep had managed to pull me under, as
frightened as I'd been. My eyes felt pickled. My bones
were heavy.

    —*Now what, sis?*

    How should I know?

    —*You look like you're waiting for something.*

    Floyd, is there something you're not telling me?

    But he went quiet.

I sat on my bed. He was right, though—I did feel like I was waiting. I just didn't know what for.

At eight o'clock my door handle moved down.

"Summer? Come on, we'll be late for school."

Wren. I ignored her. There was no way I could go to school feeling like this. I was stuck—scared to go out and scared to be in.

I heard her footsteps going down and two sets coming back up a few minutes later. I sat tight.

"Summer? Are you okay?" Dad's voice was full of concern.

I imagined telling him the truth, but even I didn't believe it. "I've got a headache," I said. It had to be stronger than that. "It feels like my brain is pressing into my skull. A migraine."

"Let me in. We'll go to the doctor."

"No. I just need darkness and quiet, Dad."

In the pause I imagined Wren mouthing something to him.

"I don't like this door being locked. Open up, Summer. I mean it."

He sounded worried enough to kick the door in, so I did as I was told. His face when he saw mine told me I looked as bad as I felt.

"Will you be all right here alone?" he said.

I nodded. "I just need to sleep."

While Dad popped into the small upstairs bathroom and rummaged for, I guessed, some headache pills, Wren stared at me and her left eyebrow shot up. That was an old trademark of hers. It meant she was suspicious. I looked away. Dad handed me two pills and I swallowed them. Come to think of it, I did actually have a headache.

Dad and Wren finished getting ready for the day and left me. When I heard the front door slam and I turned the lock of my bedroom door again, I felt a new sort of loneliness. This one had a bitter, be-careful-what-you-wish-for taste. Even loneliness had different flavors.

All day Bee lay at the end of my bed. I slept for minutes or hours at a time. Whenever I opened my eyes or moved she'd lift up her head. But she didn't nag me. Neither of us ate, but once in the afternoon I unlocked the door so I could use the toilet and Bee could run to the backyard. Afterward I locked us in again.

The day stretched on for so long that when I heard Dad and Wren come through the front door I was almost relieved.

"It's only us!" yelled Dad up the stairs. "How's the head?"

"Bit better," I yelled back. Then I heard the extra voices and groaned. First there was Julie Witkin's metallic laugh, then little footsteps unevenly running up the stairs, and finally a knock on my door. I ignored it. The handle moved down.

"Let me in, Summer. Your dad says you're sick."

"I am, Sophie. Why are you here? Didn't Dad tell you not to come up?"

"Let me in!"

"No!"

"*Seeecrets!*" She sang the word in a high-pitched tease.

I got up, hugged my duvet around me, and moved to open the door a crack, plotting how to get rid of her.

She was frowning and had her arms crossed. "There are scratches on my bike," she said darkly. "You took it again, didn't you?"

"Nope." I got back into bed and buried myself up to my neck.

"Well, guess what?" The frown had vanished. "I lost a molar!" She was fingering the gap, spit dribbling from the corner of her mouth all down her hand. In her other hand she waved a piece of paper, and let it float onto my bed. Then she plopped on a chair in the corner of the room that was covered in my clothes.

I picked up the paper. "Get better," the picture said. It was more of an instruction, like the ones she gave her mother: more biscuits, new toy, get better. She'd drawn two girls holding hands and a thick blue ribbon of sky above. We were the same height and had dots for eyes with six eyelashes above each, pretty triangle dresses, sausage legs and tiny sausage fingers, shoes as round as baby wombats, and smiles like horseshoes.

—*Be nice, Summer. She drew you a picture. And she's just a kid. She likes you.*

What would you know?

—*Hey, don't be like that with me.*

Why can't everyone *just leave me alone?*

If I ignored Sophie she'd eventually have to give up. I kept my eyes closed. Wren used to freeze me out this way all the time.

But after a while Sophie became so quiet that I got suspicious. What was she getting up to? I couldn't help it. I opened my eyes and caught her lifting the Ibanez Artwood up by its strings.

"Hey!" I snapped. "Don't touch that!"

She flinched but didn't put it down.

"I mean it, Sophie. Get away from it right this second."

"I won't break it." She frowned at me.

"I said leave it! I've got another one downstairs if you want." My birthday guitar was still propped against a wall, covered in a thin layer of dust.

"I like this one. I'll be careful, Summer. Don't boss me around." Her face was red with frustration, and she rested the guitar flat on her lap with the strings facing the ceiling. She poked four fingers in between the

D and G strings and into the sound hole, and peered in at them. Ugh! I hated this girl. Words brewed in my belly, harsh and bitter: you stupid, spoiled, thoughtless thing. You come in here, invading my space. You touch my things. You don't know anything about the world. You think it's all sunshine and magic and Christmas and the tooth fairy.

—*Summer, this isn't you.*

Yes it is, Floyd. This is how I am now.

Sophie pressed her fingers into a nothing chord on the neck and strummed messily with her right hand. She proudly flashed a gappy smile. I wanted to scream.

"Mum says I'm *very* musical."

"Good for you," I snapped.

She changed her chord into something else just as tuneless and played the strings as if she were filing her nails: strum, strum-de-strum. Then she stopped to suck her fingertips.

"Mum's getting me a clarinet." Her voice scraped over my nerves. "Or a violin. Or a cello."

—*We're going to need earplugs, sis.*

I didn't reply.

—*Don't ignore me. Please don't be like this. I miss the old you.*

I couldn't handle hearing Floyd telling me to be nice or joking with me when I was feeling so angry.

"You don't seem very sick," said Sophie.

"Well, I am."

—*Are you, though?*

"*Yes*, actually."

"What? I didn't say anything," said Sophie.

I realized I'd spoken to Floyd out loud by mistake.

"My mum says you're like this because something very sad happened to you. She won't tell me what it is. I'm too young." She pouted, like *my* thing was sad because *she* wasn't getting her own way.

"Do you want me to tell you the sad thing, Soph?"

"Yes!" she said, as if I was about to tell her how to find fairies at the bottom of her garden.

—*Be kind, Sum. She's just a kid.*

What am I, then?

I looked at Sophie's perfect little face and realized that I wanted to make her cry. I wanted to stretch her horseshoe smile into a grim, flat line.

—*This won't make you feel better, Summer.*

"My brother died," I said, as casually as a comment on the weather.

Sophie's face turned cartoon-sad with a sticking-out bottom lip. "Oh," she said. "That's so sad. What happened to him?"

—*Summer, stop. Don't tell her the details. She'll have nightmares.*

"He was in an accident."

"Oh no. . . . Our cat died last year," she said. She paused for a little while. "We're getting a new one."

It took a second for the change of topic to sink in. She thought her cat dying was the same as my brother dying. The only way she had of thinking about this was to think about herself.

But a feather-soft piece of truth floated down to me: I'd been Sophie once. Not even very long ago. I'd thought the way she was thinking now. I hadn't known that life could feel like this. I felt sorry for her and for the old me.

The hate found an exit. What would the old me have said now?

"Sorry about your cat, Sophie. We used to have a cat too."

"What was it called?"

"Charlotte. After the spider in *Charlotte's Web*."

"You named a cat after a spider?" She laughed open-mouthed like a little chimp.

For the next five minutes Sophie talked nonstop about her dead cat and all the funny things it used to get up to. I let myself fall into a kind of daze so that when I heard her clumsy plucking of the deep E string it made me jump out of my skin.

"That's too rough, Sophie! I told you before!"

"No it's not. I've seen them on *The X Factor* playing *much* harder than that."

"Sophie!" Why wouldn't she hear me? Why did she keep making me so angry?

She plucked all six strings again and I couldn't take it anymore. I was half out of bed by now and I swiped at her. "Seriously, get off, Sophie." I steadied myself, grabbed the guitar, and pushed her off the mound of clothes.

"I don't like it when you do that!" she shouted, with one hand on her hip and the other stopping traffic.

"I don't care *what* you like, you brat."

"You're not allowed to call me that! It's rude and I'll tell!"

"I'll call you what I like. And if you *ever* touch this guitar again . . ."

Sophie's bottom lip quivered, and in one swift movement she ran out. I slammed my door after her and gasped as a shock of cold air swept over my back. I froze. It's just the draught from the door, I told myself. But it had come from behind. Something had happened. I was too stiff with fear to put it into words.

I stayed in the same position, breathing in short, even sputters. My hand was flattened against the door. Blood drummed in the soft well underneath my throat as I waited for the courage to move from this moment into the next. My whole body believed something night-marish was behind me, and my brain couldn't make the monster any smaller.

There was someone in here with me.

Eyes shut. Turn around. Face the truth. Be brave, Summer.

Three.

Two.

One.

Eyes open.

There he was. The creek boy, the boy in our backyard, the boy in the dark of my room.

Not a dream or a trick of the light: the boy was here.

the other side of
a ghost

The boy's eyes popped open as if he'd been woken from a deep sleep by a loud noise. And when he'd taken in where he was, fear transformed his face and deepened as each second passed. His eyes darted around my bedroom.

I could see his fear but I could *feel* mine. So why wasn't I screaming? Why didn't I run?

I tried to listen for Floyd's voice, but it was like putting my ear to a shell. There was nothing but a *shhh* sound.

Bee got up from my bed and lay on her belly right in front of the boy, where he was sitting on the floor with his back pressed into the corner. Why did Bee trust this stranger? If he hurt her, I'd . . . Well, what *would* I do? What *could* you do to a ghost-boy? Because he had to be a ghost. How else could he be here? He wore board shorts and a dark singlet. His feet were bare. I couldn't remember what he'd been wearing the other times, but wouldn't a ghost always wear the same thing?

If I stayed still and silent, maybe he'd disappear.

He rested his forehead on his knees, his shoulders heaving as he took a few deep breaths. Then he looked up again and the same confusion passed over his face.

"I can't believe this is happening," he whispered. Finally he looked at me.

Yes, *I'm* here, I thought. This is *my* room. *My* place. You're the one who keeps showing up.

Maybe I wasn't afraid of him after all. Maybe I was just angry that he kept invading my space. Maybe fear and anger were the same thing sometimes.

He clasped his hands together. They were shaking. I held the guitar against me like a shield. Was he going to speak again? Ghost-boy, creek-boy: come on, I thought, tell me why you're here.

"What do you want?" I said.

He didn't reply and I couldn't read his face.

"Were you in my garden the other night?"

He glanced at my window and then at Bee, who now lay on her side, showing the boy her soft golden tummy. She lifted one paw and batted the air with it, as if she were waving, trying to attract the boy's attention. My brain kept flicking between how calm Bee seemed and how impossible this was. I glanced at the door and couldn't think why I was petrified that it would open again at any moment.

"You've been in my room before, haven't you?"

"I think so." His voice was hoarse, as if he hadn't used it for a while, and he cleared his throat. "It was dark. I didn't know where I was. I thought it was a dream." His excuses almost sounded like saying sorry.

"But *this* isn't a dream," I said. "I'm awake. The sun's out. It's the afternoon."

He shook his head but then shrugged, as if he'd changed his mind. The more unsure he looked, the more my anger and fright turned to frustration. Why wouldn't he tell me what was happening, what he wanted?

He looked younger than I'd thought before. Definitely a boy, not a man. Fifteen, maybe. His face was like Floyd's had been: smooth cheeks and bright eyes, lanky arms and legs that were feather-haired. And his hair was in black dreadlocks, wild and stiff like sea anemones, with hidden bits of colored wool wrapped in the depths of some of them. They ran to his jawline and he kept tucking them behind his right ear, though they were much too unruly to stay put.

His face was mesmerizing. He had brown skin with a streak of white that ran through his left eyebrow, down the middle of his eyelid, bleaching his eyelashes. It was like chalk. The iris of his left eye looked gray; the right one dark brown. Every one of his features was defined; every bone wanted you to know about it, like a sculpture.

But even though I could see what he was made of, he didn't have the solid look of the other things in my room. He looked half-here, half-not. He had to be, as I'd first thought, a ghost-boy.

"Why do you keep coming here?"

"I've got no idea. I thought *you* were making it happen."

The feeling that I'd seen him before any of this happened wouldn't go away. "When I first saw you at the river, I thought I knew you from somewhere else. Maybe I met you back home in London. Have you ever been there?"

"Never. I've never left Melbourne, not even once." He looked out the window. "We are in Melbourne, aren't we?"

I nodded, but we were getting nowhere. "What were you doing at the river that day? Was someone chasing you?"

"What's with all the questions? I didn't ask for this to happen. Get lost."

"This is *my* house. You're in *my* room. *You* get lost."

Bee got up in her ungainly way and she barked, first at the boy, and then at me.

"What's his problem?" said the boy.

"*Her*." I had a feeling that Bee didn't like us arguing. The boy got up a bit but only to his haunches. I stayed standing. Bee stayed where she was, looking down to the boy and then up to me.

"What's that smell?" he said, wrinkling his nose.

I blushed and said, "Nothing! What smell?"

"School dinners. Bleach maybe."

I couldn't smell anything and felt embarrassed. You couldn't smell your own scent as well as other people could. I remembered that Mal's house smelled of cinnamon and Gran's like a wood fire, but they probably didn't know that.

"You said your name was Sophie, right?"

"I did, but . . . it isn't. It's Summer."

"Summer. Okay. Just tell me for real, are you making this happen to me?"

"No!" I sounded so sure but I wasn't. "I can't be. Well, not on purpose. I don't know anything about . . ."

"About what?"

I didn't want to say the word "ghosts" out loud.

He pushed his finger and thumb into his eyes, trying to rub me away perhaps. Maybe he was a ghost who had taken a wrong turn. Or maybe he was new at this.

"What's your name?" I said.

"It's Gabriel. Gabe. My friends call me G."

I didn't think that could be an invitation, and my mind settled on "Gabe," which I thought suited him.

"Man, this is so messed up. What am I still doing here?" He made a cage around his head with his arms.

Bee got down and rolled right over, like I'd taught her. She lay with her legs comically bent in the air until eventually Gabe looked at her and smiled. "I like her."

"She's mine." I felt stupid for saying it, like Sophie snatching away her favorite toy. "Her name's Bee," I added.

Bee looked around at me. She knew her name but what else did she know that I didn't about this boy? She seemed to trust him straightaway. I knew what Mal would do. She'd just come out with it. "So, I guess you're . . . I mean, don't take this the wrong way, but . . . you're dead. A ghost."

Gabe looked surprised for a moment, but then he smiled and actually laughed at me. "Sorry to disappoint you but *I'm* definitely not dead. Are you?"

"Am I what?"

"Dead, obviously."

"No!"

"See how it feels?"

"Yes, but..." I wasn't going to argue now. I'd wait for him to confess. I'd be the one to hold out the longest. Floyd and Wren used to do this. They'd play tricks on me and would never let up until I said I believed them. I wasn't going to let this boy win. Whether Gabe believed it or not, he had to be a ghost. I'd been talking to Floyd since before Christmas—just a voice, though, I'd never seen him—so maybe things had gotten mixed up and they'd sent me the wrong spirit or illusion, or whatever a ghost was. Maybe that explained why I couldn't hear Floyd's voice when Gabe was around.

I couldn't make up someone like Gabe. I'd never find that detail inside myself. And I'd never seen a scar or birthmark like the one on his eye.

After what felt like ages, he said, "It's lasting longer this time. It was only about a minute when I was in the garden, the same when I was here the first time. More when I saw you at the river."

"Where did you go after I left the river? And after every other time?"

"Home, I guess? Except"—his face screwed up— "when I'm home, I don't remember this crazy stuff. Life just carries on." Suddenly his face looked terrified, as if he'd just remembered something.

"What is it?"

"What? Nothing." He seemed annoyed with me for asking, but I couldn't stop my questions now.

"Can you feel the floor?" I said.

Gabe put his hands flat on either side of him. "Why? Is there a portal under here or something?" He smiled. Every time he did, I felt I could relax a bit.

"No, I just wondered if . . . if you could *feel,* you know?"

"I can feel." He shrugged. "Look, I can pat your dog."

I froze as he reached out a hand and put it gently on Bee's head.

"There. Warm, hairy, like a dog. What did you expect?"

But that's when I knew that Gabe really couldn't be in my world, because if you ever touched the top of Bee's head she'd stop you. She didn't like it. She'd swivel her chin up to let you know that she preferred to be touched under there, or down her chest. She did it every single time, to every single person. And Bee hadn't moved a muscle. Bee couldn't feel Gabe's hand. Gabe was either imagining it or lying to me.

Then again, Bee was behaving as if she could not only see Gabe but as if she liked him, too.

"You're the best, aren't you, girl?" said Gabe. He held out his hand to her nose. She sniffed it, but she didn't lick it.

I got up nervously, and walked over to him.

"Touch my hand." I reached out, keeping as much distance between us as possible.

"Hang on. You still think I'm not real, don't you?"

"It's impossible for you to be real!" I took my hand back.

"I'm not a ghost, Summer! I'm alive. My name's Gabe. Gabriel de Souza, if you want the official version. You can look me up. I'm fifteen and I live . . . Wait, where are we?"

"It's called Fairfield."

"I live only a few kilometers from here! In a unit— not a grave or wherever you've pictured me. With a family. Well, with my mum—she's my family. I'm there every day. Every. Day. Believe me, Summer, I'm real. I'm *real*." He smacked his chest several times, and I swear I could *almost* hear the sound of it. "This is happening to *me*, got that? *I'm* the only one being shifted about all over the place. Not you."

"Don't shout. Someone will hear you."

"So what? Maybe they can help me. You won't be able to if you don't even believe I'm real. Look." He stood up and I felt small and somehow in the wrong, even though my head was telling me I couldn't be. "I can feel this wall. Your dog. Your pillow. Are you watching? One's cold, one's warm and shaggy, one's soft. I can *feel* them." He touched each one in turn, but his hand left no mark on my pillow. I kept that to myself and just stared at him. "I can feel and I *have* feelings. So I'm *real*."

He must have seen the look on my face, though, because he said, "Fine. Give me your hand, then."

My fingers were shaking. When I saw his hand up close, I watched it flicker from solid to transparent from second to second as if with every blink of my eyes he was here and then not here. When our fingers were as close as they could be, an electric shock coursed through my arm and we both pulled back.

"What was that?" he said.

"I don't know."

"Did I hurt you?"

"No, I'm fine."

"Good. This is just . . . Sorry, I can't get my head around it. But Summer, I'm real, okay?"

"Okay. I'm sorry, too." I moved my fingers, touching the tips where the calluses from playing guitar had grown again and the nerve endings weren't as sensitive. But every nerve I had remembered that electric touch.

Gabe looked like he was on the verge of tears. His expression changed when he noticed the guitar. "Is that yours?" he said, frowning.

"Yes. Can you play?"

He paused and blinked slowly, as if he'd gone somewhere in his mind. "Always wanted to. Never had one to learn on."

A new idea rose like bubbles in my mind: the guitar is part of this. At the creek, at my bedroom window, Sophie playing just now.

But before I could stretch out that thought to make any sense, Gabe started to fade.

"I think something's happening. You're going," I said.

Gabe looked at his hands, then at Bee, and then at me. "How can you tell? I can't see any difference."

I could. Gabe was spreading and fading like smoke. His arms and legs, boneless, and his face slipping and twisting away until finally there was nothing in the corner of my room but dust motes.

For a moment, my room held the echo of him. Then it exhaled and my ears popped like when we landed here in the airplane. Suddenly the sounds around me were louder: a lawnmower, and kids' voices from a nearby garden.

He was gone, but where?

I opened my door, unsure if everything on the other side would be as it was. Everything looked normal, except . . . from the top of the stairs I saw Sophie's plaits just whipping out of sight at the bottom. Had she been up here listening all that time? Would she tell?

Staying out of sight, I listened and heard Sophie crying to her mum about the way I'd shouted at her. She didn't say a word about hearing me talk to Gabe, though, so she can't have had her ear to the door. So what had she been doing all that time, then? I was sure she wouldn't waste the chance to get me into trouble after what I'd said to her.

I knew three things. One: I wasn't imagining Gabe— Bee could see him as well. Two: Gabe had to be my secret. And three: now that this mysterious thing had started, I needed to know how, and especially why.

My feelings jangled like wind chimes, hinting at change. I had to see him again, as soon as possible.

Not here, though. Not in this house, with Wren and Dad always watching me and nosy neighbors who never left us alone. But I knew just the place.

the other side of
knowing

When the Witkins left that afternoon, Dad didn't shout at me for being mean to Sophie. It was worse than that. His whole face puckered with lemon-sharp disappointment. I was glad Wren was out; I wouldn't have been able to handle her sugary sighing. The old angry Wren would have understood.

It was Dad's fault that he made it so easy for me to walk right around the back of him, while his eyes were glued to the game, and sneak out of the house without him even noticing.

I was sorry for what I'd said to Sophie because her bike was right there and the consequence of me being mean to her was that now I couldn't take it. Floyd's guitar was heavy enough to carry to the front door, let alone all the way to the creek. I cursed my puny arms and short legs, but the frustration made me stronger. I pulled the strap tighter so that the guitar felt like a new backbone, and I kept going. It would be getting dark soon and the dark was much worse in a place you didn't know very well.

Floyd's third song was folded in my pocket so that I had something to play. It was "Somewhere Only We Know," and I hummed it as I walked to distract myself from the weight of the Ibanez Artwood.

How come you never told me about the songs, Floyd?

—Some things you have to work out for yourself.

Fine, I will.

Floyd was beginning to sound like a grown-up.

My heart sank when I got within sight of the rock and I found Milo and Wren sitting there. I'd let myself think of it as my place, but of course it wasn't. I hid behind a gum tree with strips of bark that hung in curtains. They were both leaning back against the bank with sketchpads on their knees. The pile in between them that looked like tiny burned twigs was charcoal, Wren's favorite thing to draw with. From here I could see that Milo was sketching the landscape in front of him. Wren's paper was covered in faces, but I couldn't tell who they were.

I watched as Milo said something quietly and Wren laughed and playfully punched his arm. It was wrong to feel angry with people just for being happy but I couldn't deny it. I wanted to run down there and grind the pile of charcoal into the rock with my toes. I wanted to scream at Wren—though I didn't know which words would come out. My thoughts were tangled like a bagful of fairy lights.

How far would I have to walk to find a place where it was safe to meet Gabe? I crept along a higher ridge, out of sight. Walking off-map made me nervous, but there were sounds that I knew. There was the rush of the river, and the birdsong—a piercing *ting* that stabbed the air and a long *creak* that sounded like a door with rusted hinges.

I came to a grassy mound sticking out as if it were the roof of something. It looked like somewhere a hobbit would live. I went down the slope, using the trees to slow me down so I didn't end up in the river.

—*Be careful.*

I'm okay. I can do this.

The mound covered a huge stone mouth, a giant pipe that had a pitch-black gullet stretching deep into the riverbank. The end of my shoe buffeted the creek's edge, and I felt water seep into my sock. My toes curled inside my shoes.

The creek water was glassy and sage-colored, and a leaf gliding down here and there was the only sign that the river was a living, moving thing; that it could be peaceful but, secretly, powerful.

Inside the echoey chamber there were cigarette butts and squashed cans—not fresh looking, and bone dry. There were graffiti tags all over the gray walls, too, so it had to be a safe place to be at least some of the time. There was even a plastic crate I could sit on. I relaxed a bit. From here I felt hidden enough to try to get Gabe to come again. I pinned the music to the ground with an old soda can. Twice he'd come after a single string was plucked; twice after I'd played a song. At least this way if he didn't show up again I could say it wasn't for nothing—I was learning the songs Floyd had wanted to play with me.

But I did want him to show up.

This song was harder to play than the others. Or maybe I was just distracted, thinking about what Floyd's guitar could do. Each chord change made me nervous. I wondered if the way I held the guitar—or even how I felt when I played—made a difference to whether Gabe would come or not.

I played the entire song through, but it didn't work. I was angry that Sophie, in her clumsiness, had managed to make Gabe appear but I couldn't. If this was magic, it had its own mind. It wouldn't be controlled or taken over by me. It wasn't like Floyd making the cat disappear at my birthday party; the magic was making the rules. But I was determined. I started the song from the beginning.

As I reached the chorus, a shadow came over me. My heart skittered like a frightened mouse. There was Gabe's silhouette in the mouth of the pipe.

He looked shocked, like before. But even when he noticed me and the confusion washed out of his face, he didn't smile.

"I hope this is okay," I said.

"How long has it been since the last time?" Gabe's voice was low, like someone blowing softly on the top of an empty bottle.

"Not long. Why?"

"Is it the same day?"

"Of course. It was only an hour ago."

He frowned and shook his head.

"You *do* want to know why it's happening, don't you?" I said.

"Do I?" He laughed softly, not unkindly, I thought. "What if the reason turns out to be worse than not knowing?"

"I hadn't thought of that."

"No, you're right." He came a little closer and knelt on the ground. "Listen, Summer—wait, it *is* Summer, right?" He had this mischievous grin that made me realize he didn't doubt his memory of my name, but whether I'd given him the right one.

"Yes, it is."

"Summer, I wanted to say: this *is* happening to you, not just to me. It's obvious. I just got angry because . . . well, it doesn't matter, and I'm sorry."

He was scared like I was. His "sorry" was unexpected and made me think I could trust him and we could work this out together. I smiled and nodded, so we could start again.

"Where are we?" he said. "Is this a storm drain?"

"Not sure. What's a storm drain?"

"Where'd you come from again?" He smiled.

"London."

"Loads of storm drains there."

"Oh, right. Sorry, I never noticed."

"No reason to know unless you're into skateboarding or . . . drainage, I guess?" He laughed at himself.

"Do you skateboard?"

"Obsessively." He looked at the curve of the walls as if he was imagining skating up them right now. "Where's your dog? Bee, isn't it?"

"At home."

"Oh." He looked disappointed. And it seemed like it was up to me to get to the bottom of this mystery.

"This is what's making it happen." I lifted the guitar a fraction. "If I play, you show up."

"Makes me sound like some kind of genie."

"Maybe you are. Maybe I'm supposed to make some wishes." I wondered what I'd wish for. For Floyd to come back, of course. In fact, for everything to be the way it used to. For us to be back home in London. For Mum to be Mum again . . . The strangest thing was that another wish I was thinking of felt more possible than any of those: for Gabe to be real. For him to be my first real friend here maybe. It was new and awkward but that's what it felt like. Friendship. Either that or a terrifying trick the universe was playing on me.

Everything was so still and quiet now. This enormous drain had soundproofed the outside world. Hopefully it worked in reverse, too.

"What were you doing?" I said. "I mean, before I—"

"Before you summoned me with your guitar?" He was teasing again. I had the impression that he laughed his way through life, like my brother had. "I guess I was sleeping. Look." He changed position so that he was sitting with his knees bent in front of him. "Bare feet, T-shirt, comfy pants. And I have that just-woke-up feeling."

Gabe had bony feet and long toes; his trousers were much too short and there was something sort of sweet about that.

"So it can't be your dream, because you're awake," I said.

"Right. I think. Do you, um, still think I'm dead?"

I didn't want to lie to him. "I don't want you to be."

"Thanks, I guess." He looked puzzled, but he smiled.

"It's just that my brother . . . And sometimes I wonder if . . ."

He waited a bit and then said, kindly, "Summer, you need to finish one of those sentences."

I felt like I was taking one step over a cliff and was about to let myself fall. "Sometimes I think that he's talking to me. I can really hear him. This was his guitar. So I wonder if *he's* meant to be here."

"Instead of me. What happened to him? You don't have to tell me if you don't want to."

"A bomb," I said. "Waterloo."

He looked confused.

"It's a train station in London."

"Oh. I thought I'd heard that word before but I'm sorry, I don't think I ever heard about that bomb."

"That's okay."

Instead of saying all the usual things, he stayed looking at me, *really* looking, not like the people who couldn't meet my eyes once they knew. And he hadn't said anything about hearing voices or being crazy. I looked away first.

"Want to change the subject?" he said.

I nodded rapidly, and he pushed himself to standing and stretched. He rubbed his eyes roughly and I realized he was fading fast.

"Wait, you're going!" I said, panicking. "I'll play again." My fingers made a messy G major.

"I'm so tired, Summer."

"But you've only just . . . And we . . ."

"I need to sleep." He yawned. "All of a sudden I feel like I've never been this tired." He stumbled backward. I tried to grab onto his hand and we both cried out and flinched at the static touch.

"Gabe!"

But he'd gone before I'd even started my good-bye.

"Gabe!" My voice echoed.

I couldn't believe I would be leaving here without any more answers. When I was with him, I forgot to ask the right questions.

On the wall behind where Gabe had been I saw something. A capital G in a circle, sprayed in electric blue with white highlights that made it look like it had a shine. It could be any G . . . But even though he said he'd never been to the river, he also said he only lived a few kilometers from here . . .

Behind me, the dark gully rumbled from deep inside and our hideout didn't seem as friendly anymore.

I stumbled out of its mouth, landing one foot in wet mud, then struggling up the bank with one arm awkwardly angled to keep the guitar out of harm's way and the other grabbing onto long grasses and branches. Once I reached the pathway I kept running, and only slowed when I recognized that I was nearly at the rock.

In my mind I told my sister everything that was happening with Gabe. I pictured Milo the brainbox saying, "That's entirely possible. This is why . . ." and Wren putting her arm around me and taking me home, believing me. But then I became rational again, worried about my mind going bad. Maybe I was just seeing things, hearing things, and needed help.

I stopped to catch my breath. The rock was empty, and the sun was just starting to go down.

the other side of
me

The day darkened as I walked back to the house. I felt like I'd been out for ages, but it was only five thirty.

I closed the door silently, took off my shoes, and slipped into the living room across the polished floors. The football was still on. Dad hadn't moved. Between where I stood and the back of his head, secrets were growing thick like giant beanstalks.

I wriggled my toes inside my wet socks; they were proof of my adventure. I decided that tomorrow I wouldn't lie in bed and waste another day like I had today. The side of me that had been in charge since we got to Australia was a stranger to everyone I loved. Even Floyd. Gabe seemed honest and kind. I wanted him to get to know the old me, the real me.

The real me missed Dad, I had to admit. And the real me was so tired of being angry and lonely and mean. Bee was by Dad's stretched-out feet. Lately I'd stolen his friend and I hadn't thought once about how that would make him feel. I didn't want to be this way.

"Is there any dinner?" I asked in a quiet voice.

Dad spun around with a look of surprise. "On a plate in the fridge. I called up to you but you didn't answer. Wren's out but she'll be back soon. I can microwave it for you, if you like."

"Thanks, I can do it."

It was the most normal conversation we'd had in ages. In a way it was like someone else had been playing the part of Summer and now that I was trying to take over again it was awkward. I stared as the microwave hummed and the plate of vegetables with rice noodles turned. Then the noise from the TV stopped.

"Summer," said Dad, "we need to talk. I'm worried about how unhappy you are. It's not . . . not *healthy* for you."

"What do you mean?" I tried to keep my voice steady.

"I feel like I'm losing you."

Tears sprang into my eyes. I bit my lip. He worried about me, even if it was for his silly health reasons. I missed being close to him, but getting back to my old self wouldn't be as easy as turning a page or clicking my heels. I didn't even know if I'd remember *how* to get back to her. I wished that Milo could draw me a beautiful map to show me the way, but even he wasn't that clever.

"Summer? Don't you have anything to say? You won't talk to me. Or your sister. Or Gran. Or Mum."

The microwave pinged unceremoniously.

"I'm okay, Dad. You don't need to worry."

The mention of Mum made me even more scared to come out of my cocoon. But, for now, I'd take small steps. I believed I could get out of bed the next morning. I believed that my mystery—Gabe's mystery—was worth working out. It didn't matter if that was the only reason to get out of bed tomorrow.

"I just haven't been feeling well, Dad. But I'm going to school tomorrow."

"That's great, love. Are you making friends?"

"I am, yes. I promise."

I was coming around to the idea that Gabe was a real, living boy who had a house just up the road, and that I could work out the magic.

I ate every mouthful as if I'd been on space food for months; I tasted every flavor. This new feeling was like waking up after a high fever. The whole time I was shoveling noodles into my mouth, Gabe was in the back of my mind. Somewhere in that murky place

Floyd was, too. I couldn't help wondering what one had to do with the other and what I could call the force that made Gabe appear. Was it a force in my life or in his? I was going to find out.

That night, sleep was an ocean and my dream was an undertow. It sucked me underwater and roughly brought me back to shore.

———————

I'm in a house I've never been to before, standing at a kitchen counter in front of a red kettle that's whistling on the stove top. *Cold feet.* I look down to find that I'm standing barefoot on bright-orange floor tiles, and that the cold feet are not mine. I wriggle the toes. *You're a boy. This is your house.*

In the next breath I'm opening the cupboard in front of my head and taking out two mugs and a box of teabags. I feel taller and stronger in my body but tired in my heart. I'm making tea for someone. *Mum.*

Instinct guides me. Sugar in the pantry, second shelf on the right in a blue bowl with a lid and a china spoon inside. *She takes two with a splash of milk.*

"Mick?" calls a voice from the other room.

She needs you. I know she's calling for me but I also know that I am not Mick. *Mick's her brother. He's dead. She calls out for him at this time of day.* My thoughts are like single lines from fortune cookies that I read out and toss away as if I've read them before.

"Coming!" I call. The voice is familiar. *Bring her the tea. She needs to drink it so she can take her medicine.*

I pick up the mugs and just before I turn, I edge away from the cupboard and stand opposite the window above the kitchen sink. I can make out a reflection and the light catches my eyes; one dark, one light.

the other side of
time

When I woke up, I was crouched in the corner of my room: the dream I'd been having had made me sleep-walk for the first time in ages.

A storm like I'd never heard before was raging outside. I clambered back into bed and wrapped myself tightly in the covers. The sound was everywhere; wrecking balls against all sides of our house. I'd never heard thunder like that.

I watched through the window, feeling a sort of wonder at the noise. I kept drifting into a daze about the dream I'd had. It was dancing in my mind's eye like a leaf on a breeze. The harder I tried to concentrate on it, the farther the breeze blew it out of reach. Now all I remembered was being in a house and making tea. And something about feet. Nothing would stay still long enough for me to grab onto.

The branches outside fizzed and hissed in the storm. They'd bend hard in one direction and then get thrown to the other side, completely helpless. The rain came down in sheets that made the night blur. I tried so hard to stay awake, to get the rest of the dream back.

But I couldn't hold on; sleep was coming for me again.

———————

It was eerily quiet when I woke. The thunder and high winds were over, and one clear thought came to me, the last cold raindrop of the storm landing on the top of my head. The drain at the creek would be gushing with water. The song I'd left inside would be swept into the cold brown river. Every chord would dissolve and the paper would turn to mush. That would be the third song I'd lost. How could I have been so careless?

—*But you remember the notes, Summer.*

I think I do, Floyd. But still. It was a piece of you.

I dressed for school like I'd promised I would the night before, and wrote a careful note to say I'd set off early to catch up on the work I'd missed. Really all I wanted was to see Gabe again. Why had he suddenly felt so tired in the storm drain? Was it the magic? Was it a hint that it was dangerous to keep bringing him here?

I needed to bring the guitar in its case this time, because I'd be going to school straight afterward. I laid it inside very carefully, flicked down the catches, and went out the front door. The air was cold and damp, and I was carrying too much weight. The way to the creek stretched out farther. I noticed that Sophie's bike wasn't in the front garden anymore. Not that I could have used it anyway, because there was no way to balance the case, but I wondered, had I done that? It felt strange being the first person Sophie didn't trust. Maybe I also felt a little sorrier for scaring her.

I walked as fast as I could in the direction of the river. I had to stop every few strides because the case was so heavy. How was I going to make it there and back before school started? It was a quarter past eight and school started at nine, so I didn't have all the time in the world.

At the end of Lime Street, I heard a noise behind me.

"Bee!" She ran to me and sat obediently, her face almost level with mine, whipping her tail left and right across the paving stones. She nuzzled the guitar case, stood with a straight, firm back, and looked at me.

"Are you saying 'Let me help you?' Oh, Bee, you're amazing." I held one end of the case and rested the other on Bee's back. We walked along like that, carefully, at first, but then faster and faster. With Bee helping, the guitar was hardly any weight at all.

We passed the "Wominjeka" sign. I glanced at the rock and kept walking because I had to get to the storm drain. I wanted to be sure that the drain really was gushing water and that the song was truly lost. The water was tumbling forward today, but the sun was shining a bright hole through the clouds and every spider's web twinkled with raindrops.

I breathed in the earthy smell and felt something I hadn't felt in a long time: happy to be in this day. I felt lucky, too, so when we arrived at the storm drain and I saw the song was gone, the loss of it hurt but didn't stop me.

We came to a bridge that you could reach by a steep flight of stairs, only the stairs were blocked. The bridge was in two halves, with a big gap in its middle where the two ends didn't meet anymore. The drop-offs and the staircase entrance were bound in bright orange plastic fencing to stop anyone getting hurt. There was nowhere to go but back where I'd come from—or I could get underneath the bridge and tuck myself under the staircase.

"Come on, Bee, down here." Carefully we walked down the bank to a steep dark slope and a space big enough for two people and a big dog.

I sat quite close to the water, but still hidden from the path, on top of the empty guitar case because the ground was damp. The new song was "Wish You Were Here." So far this was the only one I didn't know, and it made my playing awkward because I couldn't hear how it was supposed to sound in my head. I played it all the way through, badly. And then again.

"Where is he, Bee?"

She looked intently at the guitar as if she knew what I was trying to do. I concentrated hard and played the song again.

"Behind you."

I gasped and looked around. Gabe was tucked right up the slope. "I've always liked this spot."

"You have? I thought you'd never been to the river."

He frowned. "I did say that, didn't I?" He clambered down toward me. Once he'd reached the water's edge, he bent down and pointed upstream, in the direction where the path ended. "Look above the treetops, over there. See that tower block in the distance? I live on the top floor."

"Wow, just there. But wait, hang on—why did you tell me before that you'd never been to the river?"

"Don't make it a big deal. I forgot."

"Fine," I said, frostily.

"I wasn't lying."

"It's okay. Forget it." The old me would have trusted him. "Do you come here a lot, then?"

"Used to. Don't have time these days, to be honest."

"What, school and things?"

"Not school. Things."

A phrase popped into my head: *her medicine.* Where had that come from? An image swam in front of my eyes: a red kettle boiling on the stove top. Wasn't that from my dream? I pushed it aside.

"Hey, it's my friend Bee," said Gabe. He lifted his hand to say hello, and Bee got down on her front legs and stretched her back with her bottom in the air, which was a "hello" she usually only did for me or Dad.

"That means she trusts you."

"We had a dog when I was little. A pug. But that was before . . . Nothing. Anyway, I've just thought of something Dad and I used to do here years ago. I'll show you."

I wanted to ask what he'd been about to say, but the moment had gone. Now I was curious about what he would show me. He went to a tree that was sticking out at an angle over the water, right next to the bridge. It looked like he was trying to tear off a piece of bark. The piece he was grabbing at hadn't moved, and I watched his confusion. He still thought he was here the same way I was.

197

"I can't get it," he said.

"Here, let me pass it to you." I tore off the piece and he held out his hand. I hesitated; we were standing so close now. I dropped the bark toward his hand, but in the blink of an eye it was on the ground.

"But I felt it," he said.

"Maybe it's just because you know what it *should* feel like."

"Maybe." He looked disappointed.

"You can talk me through it instead."

"That'll have to do."

"Do you think we'll have time? Before your alarm goes off or your mum wakes you up and you fade away?"

"My mum wouldn't . . ." He cut the sentence dead.

Gabe didn't completely trust me.

"Do you still not remember anything about this when you're awake?" I asked.

"I don't think about it at all. It's like I forget."

"Oh. Well. That's fine." It was definitely not fine. I thought about nothing else.

Just when I was building up my defenses, another odd phrase popped into my head: *two sugars*. I'd been making tea in the dream. The sugar was in the blue bowl.

"It doesn't mean I don't want to be here, Summer. I'm not even scared anymore, for some reason. It feels like I should be here. Does that make sense to you? 'Cause it sure as hell doesn't to me."

"Come on." I tried to be in the moment and picked up the piece of bark from the ground. "Tell me what I'm supposed to do with this."

I got more bark, twigs, and a collection of differently shaped leaves. We sat on the slope and Gabe showed me how to make little boats. It reminded me of Floyd teaching me the guitar, which hadn't been like when Mum taught me long division and kept shifting in her seat when I took too long, or when Dad let me help make a birthday cake and took over when I couldn't hold the mixing bowl still. Gabe spoke to me like he believed without a single doubt that I could do it. For the first time in ages, I didn't feel small.

As I worked away, we talked. I told Gabe about Wren and Milo. How they'd become close and what a strange thing it was because of the way Wren used to be. He laughed at my impression of her and seemed to understand why the new, nice version made me grind my teeth.

I told him about Sophie, though I found that when I came to the part about yelling at her, I felt awful and changed my story.

Gabe was a good listener, and when he spoke he chose his words carefully. I felt as if mine were pouring out too fast, like a kid with a giant cereal box, making a mess everywhere.

He talked about his friends—Ajay, Coop, and Blake—in a way that reminded me of Floyd and his gang. Floyd's friends were like his brothers.

Gabe told me funny stories from when he was little, like the time he got completely stuck in a chair and it had to be sawed apart to free him. And the time he broke his leg jumping off a bridge as high as the one we were sitting under.

He said he used to spend lots of time much farther up the river, when he was younger and his dad was still around. They'd look for Christmas beetles and blue-tongue lizards, and I laughed because those sounded too good not to be made up. He told me there were snakes by the river, too, and I couldn't help checking around me.

"Don't worry, too cold for them now. Seasonal, like my dad."

"Where does he go?"

"No idea. He never says. Can't hack family life. It's been a year since the last time he left."

"Don't you hate him for that?"

"No. Tried that. Waste of time." He shrugged. "What's the point?"

"I don't know what the point is. But I just can't help it with my mum."

"What did she do?"

"She left us. Well, she made us leave her, but it's the same thing. We were all supposed to come to Australia together, but suddenly me, Dad, and Wren were on the plane without her, with no explanation. She wanted to get rid of us all along. After Floyd died she didn't want to love us anymore. It was too hard for her."

Gabe nodded calmly. After the anger had risen as I told him things I'd never said out loud before, it lay back down again. I felt like I'd taken a giant breath. So I thought, what if Gabe's here to help me? What if that's the point of this? The universe was always matching people up with a perfect friend—like me and Mal—or making them come across a piece of knowledge that completely changed their life. Maybe it was just trying out something new on me.

In a shimmer of light like the sun catching a mirror, I finally saw a proper picture of what I'd dreamed last night. Making tea. Two sugars. His mum calling out a different name: "Mick." She had to take her medicine. It was Gabe's house I'd imagined.

I was scared to say this to him, as if I'd been trespassing in his life and finding out things he didn't want me to know.

"Hey, shouldn't you be at school by now?" Gabe pointed at my blazer.

"Oh my God, school! How long have we been here?" My feet had gone dead underneath me, like thick cushions. Bee stood with her head bent low so I could lean on her to get up. I grabbed my guitar and stumbled a little way down the slope. Gabe reached for my arm to stop me falling and we both flinched as usual.

"Sorry!" we said.

"What will I do here without you?" he said. "I thought we were going to have a boat race."

I put the guitar in its case. "If I don't go to school, Dad and Wren will get suspicious. I'm really sorry."

"I'm just messing. I guess I'll disappear soon, anyway," he said. "Back to bed where I belong."

I didn't believe that he spent all day in bed. He was hiding something. And I didn't want to leave him. I liked the way he always put his hair behind his ears, even though it would never stay. I liked that I'd never seen anyone who looked quite like him. I liked how being here made me feel.

The more I thought about how I didn't want to leave him, the more I realized that I actually *couldn't*. That it was a real force, as real as not being able to lift both feet off the ground at once.

A terrifying thought was brewing. What if I was stuck here? What if it was like what Gran used to say when we pulled funny faces? "If the wind changes, you'll stay like that."

"I can't go, Gabe."

"I told you, I'll be fine. You shouldn't miss school."

"You don't understand. It's like I'm trapped. And listen."

"To what?"

"Exactly. No sounds. No birds." I couldn't even hear the steady rush of the water. "We can't sail your boats. See? The river is dead still." I looked at my watch; the hands weren't moving. "Gabe. Time has stopped."

the other side of Courage

I don't think either of us knew what to do, so I was relieved when Gabe broke the silence.

"My mum used to believe in spiritism. She would have said that's what this is. Except one of us would need to be the spirit."

"Not me." I smiled.

"Not me either. See this mark through my eye? When I was little and people teased me about it, Mum would tell me I was kissed by a spirit. Believing in spirits was in her bones."

" 'Was'? Does that mean . . . ?"

"No," he snapped.

"Sorry, Gabe." I'd touched a nerve and changed the

mood. I wanted it back again. "I like your eye. I think it looks cool. Did you believe in the spirit?"

"For as long as I could, because it helped when I got called 'mutant' all the time. But then I read up on the science of it and I found out that we're all mutants in some way, and that helped too. Even you, with your blue eyes."

"I am?"

"Sure. Blue eyes are a ten-thousand-year-old mutation. Before that, everyone had brown eyes. So I reckon someone will be able to explain what's happening to us one day, the way we can explain genetics now and couldn't hundreds of years ago."

"Maybe. But don't you want to know more than how? Don't you want to know why?"

When I thought about telling him that the why might be so he could help me, I realized how that would sound. And surely there had to be more to it than that. What was in it for him?

"Gabe, I know you said this wasn't like any dream you'd had before, but what if that's exactly what it is? You could be asleep right now, and dreaming, except that what you're dreaming is also real." I remembered the fragments of my own dream last night: what was happening to Gabe could also be happening to me. "You're dreaming outside of your mind instead of inside."

"I am? That sounds . . . Wait, I need to get my head around what that means. What I don't get is, why you?"

"Why me what?"

"I didn't mean it to sound like that. I meant, why *us*? It's good that it's you. Whoever you are." He smiled.

I had to tell him as much as I could about my dream. "I think I went to your house, Gabe."

"That's impossible . . . Why didn't you tell me? When?"

"In a dream, I mean."

He looked worried. "What did you see?"

"Not much. I was making tea. Is your sugar kept in a blue bowl? One of the mugs had a tiger on it." The more I told him, the more of my dream I could see.

"That's my mug. The Tigers. My football team. But . . ."

"The other said 'Best Mum in the World.' In pink."

He swallowed. "Yes, that's hers. Did you see her? Did she speak?"

"She called out for someone. Mick?"

He nodded, and looked as spooked as I felt.

"Who's Mick?" I said.

"Uncle. Mum's big brother. Miguel. He brought her over when she was little and pretty much raised her himself. He's dead now. Mum's got . . . Mum's got dementia so she forgets things like that. Sometimes she's all right but mostly she's not really here. I left school to look after her when Dad left."

"Oh, Gabe."

"Don't pity me!" He was angry but only for a split second. "Sorry. She just has all these holes in her memory. They get bigger every day. So when I couldn't remember coming to the river before, and when it's obvious that I don't remember what we talk about once I'm at home with her, or even that this magic thing happens, I worry that . . ."

He didn't have to finish. He was worried that the gaps in his memory were because he had the same illness as his mum. Gabe was brave but it was dressed differently from the courage I'd loved in my brother. It was soft and quiet and didn't need or want anyone to know.

"I don't think that's why you've forgotten things. If we're really dreaming our way into each other's lives . . . Well, it's normal to forget bits of your dream. That'll be why. Trust me."

From the look on his face, I saw that I hadn't convinced him.

"Are you angry with me?" I said.

"For what? What could I be angry with you for?"

"For being in your house."

"No. I trust you. Anyway, I've been in yours."

But it wasn't quite the same thing because I'd *been* Gabe in the dream, looking down at his—at *my*—feet, seeing his reflection—*my* reflection—in the glass. I'd been in his skin.

"Summer," he said, "I think you should come to my house for real next time."

the other side of
normal

After we made a plan, I watched the image of Gabe come apart like dandelion seeds scattered after one blow. The river sounds rolled around in my ears. Our bubble had burst. The minutes were on the move again and so was the river and the breeze.

Bee and I went back along the river path the way we'd come, with the weight of the guitar case between us, but at the main road she suddenly stopped.

I took the guitar case off her back and bent down to stroke her chest. "What is it?"

She licked the end of my nose and while I was laughing and wiping it clean she sped off. I understood: Bee was taking herself home—she knew the way by now—and I was to go on to school.

I walked to school slowly, as if that would help me hold on to the feeling I had after being around Gabe. It would be strange to be among all the other kids and their normal everyday routines when no one had a clue what was happening to me. To Gabe and me.

But once I got there I realized I was seeing them all as if for the first time. I wondered what was going on in all of *their* lives. What secrets did they have? What kept them awake at night? I'd been looking out of such a tiny window for so long. Now I could see a wider view.

—*That's more like it, Sum.*

It doesn't mean I don't still miss you, Floyd.

—*I know. But I don't want to be the reason you're never happy again.*

If I was going to try—really try—I couldn't talk to Floyd in my head all the time. It was like listening to one song coming from my left earphone and a completely different one in my right. I had to choose one song—the here and now song—and it took everything I had to do that.

But I managed all through first period, and second.

When recess came around, as usual Becky said, "Do you want to hang out with us today?"

"Sure," I said.

I swear she almost did a double take.

As I followed her out to the oval, she kept looking at me. I realized it wasn't fair, how hard she'd had to try just to get one "yes."

I lurked on the edge of her group of friends. I didn't talk, but I don't think Becky minded. The other girls probably wondered what I was suddenly doing there. I was in their life like Gabe was in mine, slipping in like a ghost.

Recess wasn't so bad. I could do that again, I thought.

———

I ate dinner with Dad and Wren. It was a perfectly normal scene, like turning on the TV and finding a series you used to be hooked on but haven't seen for a while. They talked; I ate and nodded in the right places. It wasn't natural, exactly, but it was easier than I'd been imagining all the times I'd made excuses not to be in the same room as them. I even wondered if the truth about Gabe would spill out of me, so I kept my lips shut tight. If the magic came out, I'd never get it back. Everyone would take a bit of it.

There was only one person who'd understand, but it had been so long, and the kind of sorry I'd have to say was too horrible to face. I tried to find that tiny seed of resentment I'd felt in London, when I'd wondered why I had to be at Mal's the night before we lost Floyd forever, but it wasn't there.

I started an email to her. "Dear Mal, I'm so sorry for not writing to you." "Dear Mal, you won't believe what's happening." "Dear Mal, there's this boy . . ." No. Delete, delete, delete. An hour later I still had nothing.

I went to sleep with whirring thoughts of Gabe and Mal and Becky and Floyd, all of them separate in real life but hanging out together in my head. My dream was a strong current that swept me all the way back home.

———

I'm in a train station. Underground. It's teeming with people, like it's a giant anthill. Everyone's on a mission, but I'm moving to a different time. My seconds tick slower than theirs.

You're dreaming. Am I? This looks too normal for a dream.

I get onto a train, but something gets trapped in the closing doors and I look back to find I'm carrying a skateboard. I wrench it out and check for damage. I notice a helmet in the crook of my arm. I look at my hands. *Are these really your hands?* I use one of them to put my hair behind my ears, but it pops straight out again.

The rhythm of the train is like a dance track

chorus—get there, get there, get there, get there—but these faces look too miserable for dancing. The journey ends and the ants pile out.

It's a relief to be aboveground. I look up at the sun and feel as if I haven't seen it for a long time.

I arrive at my final destination without remembering the journey from the station. It seems like I only blink and then I'm inside an indoor skate park. I've read about this space. It used to be huge underground tunnels but someone converted it. In the same breath I think: *You've wanted to go here for ages* and then, *Can you even skate?*

I'm at a counter opposite a man with giant plugs in both earlobes. I'm thinking about getting one of those. *You are?*

"You a friend of theirs?" he says.

Another skip in time: I'm up on a concrete ramp. There are four boys over on the other side, looking at me. Maybe they're looking because this is their place and I don't belong, maybe it's my face, or maybe it's neither of those things.

I know how good I am and I'm not going to let them put me off when I've come all this way. I drop into the ramp.

After the first rush of adrenaline, the other kids become shadows on the walls except for this one guy who's just as good as I am. Then it's just me, him, and the boards: drop in, pump, backside 50-50. Drop in, pump, ollie to fakie. I get flashes of surprise at how good I am, and in the next moment I feel like I'm about to lose control and break my neck.

Suddenly there's no board under me and I'm flying. My hip and shoulder slam against hard ground.

"You okay, man?" A voice shouts into the bowl and it bounces off every surface. Then his face is right in front of mine. It's the boy who was skating with me. He has freckles like pinpricks and red patches on his cheeks from skating. There's a smear of dirt down one of them and his hair is stuck up with sweat.

He holds out his hand and I don't know what to do so I shake it, and he laughs and pulls me to my feet.

"We'd better get out of the way," he says as a shadow-kid zooms past us. "I'm Floyd."

"Gabe," I say. "My friends call me G."

I feel suddenly claustrophobic. I wipe my arm across my burning-hot forehead.

"Here." Floyd walks over to the place where he and his friends have stashed their bags. He hands me an open can of ice-cold soda and I gulp it till the bubbles are like iron filings in my throat.

I can see his mates giving me odd looks, but Floyd's face is as friendly and trusting as any face I've ever seen.

"Is that yours?" I ask, pointing at a guitar propped against the wall. It's beautiful, a blood moon in the middle of a dark sky.

"Yeah. You play?"

I shake my head. Suddenly there's nothing I want more than to play that guitar.

"Come on, I'll teach you if you show me your ollie to fakie," he says. "Which is awesome, by the way."

"Cheers, brother," I say. Brother. My brother. I put the can down and pick up my board, but when I next look up, every figure is a shadow. They dart around like insects, and no matter how hard I try I can't find Floyd.

———————

When my eyes slowly came unstuck from sleep, I found myself curled up on the end of Wren's bed. Her feet shifted just above my head. I could hear Bee panting somewhere in the darkness. I rolled off silently and tried to slink away, so drowsy that if I moved slowly maybe I could return to the dream.

"Summer? Is that you?" Wren whispered.

"Sh." I slipped away.

the other side of
the door

In the morning I was relieved to wake up in my own bed. I hoped Wren wouldn't remember that I'd been in hers.

The first thing I thought about was the dream. Parts of it were as clear as a movie but the rest was patchy, full of dark blobs of people and places. I knew I'd been on the train, so it had to be London. I was skateboarding and I'd fallen, but had I been Gabe or had I been me? The more I tried to reach for details, the more they slipped away.

Next I thought of my unfinished emails to Mal. If I'd had the courage to send one of them, I might have had one from her by now. That is, if I could dare to think she would ever speak to me again. I got out of bed and pulled out the bottom drawer where I'd stashed the three parcels Mal had sent. She'd wrapped them so tightly that I had to find scissors to cut them open.

—So that makes me your third thought, now?

Floyd, no. It's just . . . I haven't forgotten you. Don't think that.

—I'm kidding, Summer. You know me, and I know you. Now open those parcels, would you?

I gulped and a few tears escaped but I concentrated on what I was doing.

In each parcel there was a book and a note. In the first the note said, "Because our friendship is past, present, and future. No matter what. First: the past. Look out for the next one! Love, Mal x"

The first book was a battered copy of *Charlotte Sometimes* by Penelope Farmer. It smelled musty like Gran's laundry room and looked like it had been read lots of times. As I held it, I remembered what books had felt like to me before Floyd died. Like friends.

The second note simply said, "The present. Love, Mal x" and the book was *Goodbye Stranger* by Rebecca Stead. It was a brand-new copy and smelled like glue and paper and ink.

So the third book meant "the future," and that's what the note said, too. It was a homemade book.

217

The front cover was filled with stick-figure drawings of two girls—one small and one tall—doing every kind of activity, around a title written in 3D lettering: *A Day in the Life of Summer and Malinda.*

Relief and shame swirled in my tummy. I wanted a future friendship with Mal so much. I promised myself that I would send her the best story she'd ever read in return. But first I had to work out how it was going to end.

———

At school that day, every time I thought about Gabe's apartment building my heart lurched and I lost track of the lesson I was in. I felt conspicuous, even though I'd done such a good job of making myself into the Invisible Girl.

Though, not invisible to everyone.

"Hey, Summer, I'm going to this bookshop after school." Becky grabbed my arm in the corridor and pushed a piece of paper in front of my nose. It had a picture of an author and details of a book-signing event.

"Um...That sounds...fun?" I didn't know if it was an invitation or she was just telling me she was going.

"I can never pronounce the author's name. You're good at French. How do you say it?"

"Lar-bal-est-ee-air, I think?"

"Great. So you'll come, yes?"

"I, well, I . . ." My mind went blank. I couldn't think of a single excuse. "Yes?" It just slipped out.

Becky looked so happy that I couldn't back down. What did she see in me? I was still blushing as she ran off to her final class.

We met up after school and set off toward the bookshop.

Gabe and I had agreed on five o'clock. I'd thought that having something to do before I went to find him would stop me feeling so nervous, but now I was anxious about being out with a maybe new friend. What if I said something stupid? What if I couldn't think of anything to say at all? My brain felt like it was being dissolved by acid nerves, sloshing and hot inside my skull even though it was only fifteen degrees outside.

"Can we stop at the milk bar for a drink?" I said.

"At the what?"

"Milk bar. Isn't that what it's called?" My heart squeezed tight. "It's what my dad says."

"Cool. Well, I've never heard that in my life, but it's cute. I like it! Let's go to the milk bar." She winked at me.

I felt ridiculous, even though Becky wasn't the sort of person who'd make fun of anyone. Dad said *everyone* called it a milk bar back when he was a kid growing up here. But things changed. Maybe things had already changed back home, in London. Maybe I'd go back one day and there would be new words for things, and everyone I knew would be different, and then I'd feel like I didn't belong here *or* there.

—*There's another way of looking at it.*

Floyd, you're here! Please stay. I can't do this.

—*You're okay. Listen. You* said *the words "milk bar,"*

Exactly! And Becky hasn't even heard of it!

—*Dad would have loved hearing you say that, even if it did turn out to be extinct. Think about that.*

Floyd was right. My heart unclenched. It was just a word. And I missed pleasing Dad. I missed knowing that I was special to him.

We arrived outside the bookshop and Becky grabbed my arm and gasped. "I'm so nervous."

"Of meeting the author?"

She nodded rapidly, wide-eyed.

"Becky, she'll love you. I mean, you're great." I wasn't lying; she was. Becky knew how to talk to anyone. She opened her mouth; words came out! She didn't know how magical that was to people like me.

She turned and hugged me. I held my breath and

squeezed my eyes shut and very softly rested my hands on her back.

"You're great too," she said.

I am? I thought.

We went inside. It was gorgeous: cool and dark with the smell of wood and furniture polish and books stretching around two corners, inviting you to go exploring. Becky had brought a whole stack of books for signing and they all looked like they'd been read more than once. In fact, it looked like they'd been through some terrible times—or brilliant times, depending on how you looked at it. One of them looked like it had even been dropped in the bath.

"Do you read much?" she said.

"I used to. I'm going to start again."

"These. Are. Seriously. The. Best," she said, and then she started explaining the story.

It was a series about magic, of all things: a door that led between two places that were geographically thousands of miles apart. The first one was called *Magic or Madness.* I wanted to laugh. The universe was playing all kinds of pranks on me. It took me back to the last time I'd really laughed with Mal—our wormholes conversation on Christmas Eve. I thought about the doorway I'd wanted between home and Melbourne. I thought about how somehow Gabe and

I had found doorways into each other's lives. Only, at the moment it felt like it wasn't the same door we were using.

"You like all that kind of stuff, then?" I asked. "Magic and fantasy?"

"Love it. Can't live without it."

"Do you . . . I mean, obviously not, but do you ever think magic is real?"

"You are so cute." She smiled.

I must have looked hurt because she put her arm around me and added, "I believe in it when I'm inside the book, if the book is a good one. One hundred percent. But when the story is over and I'm outside it again, I don't. That's probably why I'm always reading." She held up her stack. "Better get in the line. Want to come with me?"

"You go. I'll look around."

Becky left me to it. For the first time in ages it felt good to be around lots of people, knowing that I had a secret place of my own to go to (the creek) and someone special to share it with (Gabe). Slowly I was making my own map of this place. And in only—oh, help, half an hour—I might be seeing Gabe outside of our bubble, here in the real world.

Maybe.

Maybe.

Because my new fear was that I'd find his house and he'd open the door and not know who I was.

———————

As we left the bookshop, Becky hugged me again. It was still strange.

"What was that for?" I giggled, trying not to squirm out of her arms too obviously.

"Nothing! Just to say thanks for coming with me."

"Thanks for . . . making me."

We both laughed. Becky picked at something on my sweater. "Hey, look, you're worth $34.99."

I smiled and peeled the price sticker off the tip of her finger. "I'm expensive."

"I think you're worth it."

While I blushed, a tram hurtling along caught Becky's eye, and she started to run for it.

"See you tomorrow, Summer!" she shouted behind her.

When she said my name my lungs took an extra big gulp of air. And as I stuck the price sticker onto my English folder I realized that without me noticing, Becky Wong had burrowed her way in a tiny bit.

I walked up the high street toward Gabe's neighborhood. It was 4:55 p.m. and the sun was going down, leaving a purple dusk and drifts of pink cotton candy clouds. The streets were quieter now that the school traffic was over. I couldn't help checking behind me every few strides. Although we'd been able to see Gabe's building from the river, I couldn't see the river from here and didn't even know which direction it was in.

It suddenly hit me that no one on the whole planet knew where I was. I was scared.

—*But I know where you are, Sum. I always did, remember? When we'd play hide-and-seek?*

Yes, I remember.

I kept going, smiling at the memory of Floyd finding my hiding spots, putting his finger to his lips, and walking away to find Wren instead, so that I wouldn't always lose the game.

Stiff grass brushed against my leg as I walked up a pathway to the entrance of Gabe's building. Now that I was up close, it looked so much bigger. It towered over me, solid and grim, and I was nervous again. There was a small, empty playground on one side of the path and the wind was moving the swings back and forth. Half of the windows were lit up and half were black. There was only one light on the top floor—Gabe's floor.

I pushed one of the heavy double doors using my whole body, and once I got inside I wiped my feet on a huge mat while I tried to figure out the way to go. There was an elevator straight in front of me, or a staircase tucked away in the corner. The elevator doors opened, and a man holding hands with two cute children walked out. He smiled as they passed me. The lift didn't smell very good even from here, but the stairwell was cold and gray. The wind whistled through it and there were at least twenty floors. I got in the lift and pressed the button.

At the top there were two ways I could go, so I chose left because I remembered that Wren was left-handed and she was always complaining that left got a worse deal than right. I went down the hallway, trying to peer into windows without looking like a burglar. None of the kitchens I peered into looked like the one in my dream, but a feeling that I might be nearing the end of an even bigger journey kept me going. On top of that, the view from up here was amazing and the sunset made everything so beautiful and mellow. Together they made me feel like anything was possible.

A few footsteps later I'd found the one. Yes, I realized, breathing frantically, this was the kitchen I'd visited in my dream. The orange floor. The pantry. The small stove with the red kettle on top. Everything was in its place. Peering closer, cupping my hand to the glass, I could see the room behind, where I'd taken the tea, through a wide doorway with no door. There was a square beige carpet peeling up at the corners like a slice of stale bread. The television was on. I saw a small glass coffee table with a cup of tea resting on a coaster. Someone's feet on a footstool. The rest of their body tucked away behind the wall. I breathed on the glass and drew a G in the mist. "Please be here," I whispered.

The woman who answered the door was hardly taller than me. First she smiled at me, and then she looked confused.

"Where is Yana?"

"Um, I don't know. Are you Mrs. de Souza?" This had to be Gabe's mum. She looked a lot older than mine, but I could see she had been beautiful.

"Yana is coming!" she shouted, putting her hand up in front of my face. I'd scared her, and I wasn't used to that feeling. No one was scared of me.

"I'm so sorry. I'm a friend of Gabe's. Gabriel." I thought she'd probably like his full name, like most mums.

Again, she looked confused.

"Is Gabriel here?" I asked. I tried to raise my voice a little and say it over her shoulder, in case he was in his room. His mum was scanning my face as if she was looking for something in particular, but no matter how many times I said his name her face didn't give me any clues that she knew who I was talking about.

"Why did they send someone new? Where is Yana?"

"Sorry, I don't know. Is Gabriel here?"

Suddenly she smiled. "You have come to see the baby! Ah!" And she grabbed my arm and pulled me inside.

I was terrified; this was really being inside Gabe's home, not just a dream. What if Gabe came out of his room, or came in the front door behind me, and didn't recognize me? I would just be a stranger, a trespasser.

His mum let go of my arm and wandered off down a small, dark hallway. She went into the bathroom and closed the door. I looked around me. The place was tiny and there was hardly any light. I could see one bedroom, dimly lit, with a floral bedspread and thick pink carpet. The other two doors were closed.

I heard the shower turn on. What was Gabe's mum doing? Why would she let a stranger inside her house and then take a shower? I had to get out. Gabe was obviously not at home and I was scared. Everything was spinning out of my control.

But I couldn't leave without knowing more than I did when I arrived. I turned a door handle and found not a room but shelves full of towels and sheets. I tried the only other one. Instantly I knew this was Gabe's room. It was as if I'd had a dream about it but instead of turning into pictures, the dream had turned into a sensation like goosebumps. The walls were cold blue and there were pockmarks from posters like I remembered from my walls when we left our old house. I looked for other signs and began to notice strange things. A tube of hand cream on the bedside table, an old-fashioned patchwork quilt that looked homemade folded at the end of the bed. A bag of knitting. This was Gabe's room, but who did this stuff belong to?

I went back into the hallway and the bathroom door opened. Gabe's mum was standing in front of me in her underwear.

I panicked. Gabe had told me that she got confused and forgetful, but now that it was happening I couldn't think of the right thing to do. I went back into Gabe's room, grabbed the quilt, and put it around his mum's shoulders.

"What is this?" she said, fingering the quilt but not questioning why I was putting it around her.

"I have to go. I'm so sorry."

I left her there, not knowing what else to do, terrified of being discovered, embarrassed for her, and ashamed of myself for feeling that way. I closed the front door behind me and ran down the stairs, all the way down to street level, until my lungs were tiny and airless.

The swings were still empty, so I sat on one to catch my breath. I couldn't go home yet. What if I'd done something that put Gabe's mum in danger? What if she went back into the shower and slipped? What if I'd really frightened her? What would Gabe think of me right now?

It was soon completely dark. I was still on the swing, and shivering. I had almost gone back up a few times to see if Gabe's mum was all right, but I was scared I would make things worse. How did he look after her every day when she didn't even know his name? We had both lost our mums, in a way, but at least mine might not be gone for good. It made me want to help Gabe, somehow.

I looked up again at the building and worked out which window was his. The kitchen light was on; his bedroom was dark. Every figure who passed me by was him until a sign told me it wasn't—wrong height, wrong hair, too old. Then I saw a tall, broad woman wheeling a shopping cart go into the front entrance. I bet myself that this was Yana. I crossed the road so I could see right up to the top floor. A short while later, Gabe's bedroom light came on.

Gabe might have lived here once, but he didn't anymore.

I kept coming back to the thought that if Gabe really didn't know that, it must mean that he *was* a ghost and he couldn't remember his own death. What if my role was to prove that to him? What kind of a job was that?

Well, I wouldn't do it. What if I did tell him? And then what? It was better I didn't; that way we could carry on being friends. The way we were was fine; nothing needed to change.

There was no one else around. It was dark and Dad had just sent a worried message asking when I'd be home. A lie slipped out easily—*Still with Becky. Home very soon.*—but it curdled in my tummy. I pictured Dad smiling at the thought of me with a proper friend, took one more look up at where Gabe should have been, and walked away.

the other side of the moon

School the next day went slowly. I spent recess and lunch with Becky and her friends again, but Floyd's voice kept creeping in and I couldn't shake this heavy feeling.

—*You have to keep looking for answers.*

Why can't you just tell me them?

—*You think I know more than I do, Sum.*

I sat out on the porch in the evening, trying to read the first book Mal had sent me. I looked up when a familiar ball-bouncing sound echoed along Lime Street.

"Hey, stranger," said Milo. His hair was swept right back instead of hiding half his face. I thought how familiar he seemed now, and how his face was one of the few that I felt relieved to see every day. Milo wasn't like Gabe, but he was real and right here. I felt a pang of envy that Wren, who had spent most of her years on earth being mean, had this kind, smart, *real* friend who thought so much of her. A boy who drew reliable maps to places. "How's life?" he asked.

"Fine."

"Great."

"It's not really fine."

"No."

"Could you tell?"

"A bit. Do you want to talk about it?"

I walked over, reached for a fence post, and chipped away some white paint with my fingernail. "I'm not sure how to. You wouldn't believe me."

"Believe you? Of course I'd believe you." He waited, quietly.

"Do you believe in ghosts?" I said.

His eyes grew wider in surprise, but afterward I could tell that he was actually thinking hard about it. "It's difficult for me to say no flat out," he said. "I mean, I think there are infinite possibilities in this universe. We're only a tiny part of it. Take the stars, for example."

I couldn't help smiling because Milo sounded like a professor. "Sorry. Yes, the stars. Go on."

"Well, look up. See that one, just to the right of that peppercorn tree?"

I pretended I knew which tree was a peppercorn, but I was pretty sure I had the right star anyway. "Got it."

"Okay. That star you're seeing in this exact moment might not even exist anymore."

"What? Why? I can see it."

"But what you're seeing is the energy it sent out to reach you from millions of miles away. By the time it gets to you, time has moved on. It's a new moment. Things have changed. Maybe the star isn't a star anymore. Maybe it's gone out."

"But . . . No! It can't . . . That can't be true." I felt like he was confirming that Gabe didn't exist anymore. That he was gone from the earth like Floyd.

"Summer, I didn't mean to upset you."

I left him without another word and ran down the path, thinking I might cry. Wren opened the front door unexpectedly, and I barged past her.

"Was that Milo?" Wren closed the door. "Are you crying, Summer?"

"No." I wiped snot from under my nose. I couldn't fall apart again. "He's great, Milo is," I said in a horrible voice that nearly choked me. I wanted to hurt Wren. Make her feel unsure. "I think he really gets me."

—*Summer, don't do this. This isn't you.*

233

"Yes, he's . . . cool," Wren said too casually, her true feelings wiggling out like soft tentacles.

"He made me the most amazing map. I think I'll try to spend more time with him." The words were dripping out of me, but then so were tears. I was pathetic. "That's okay with you, right? If I spend time with Milo?"

"Sure. I don't own him." She looked sorry for me, which made me hate her even more.

"That's what I thought."

I went upstairs full of fury that couldn't find the right way out. I lay curled on my bed. I couldn't settle. I wanted to wriggle out of my skin. My mind was racing. I'd done nothing to help Gabe yet. He believed he was alive. But someone else was living in his room. What Milo had said—about the stars—meant that Gabe might be coming to me from his past.

And the one thing I had left of my brother—his precious Ibanez Artwood—was our connection. The guitar had survived for a reason, and being scared of the truth wasn't a good enough excuse to ignore it.

I got out of bed with the energy of a single thought: go to the place that felt like it was ours, even though it had belonged to thousands of people before us.

the other side of
the bridge

Bee knew exactly where we were going. She trotted ahead of me, looking back to make sure I was following.

At first I was terrified, being out so late by myself, the sky gaping over us like a black hole. But Bee was more than an average dog, and every time I thought about going back and lying in my bed, no closer to the truth, I just got faster and more determined. The Ibanez Artwood felt lighter on my back.

I couldn't explain what was making me go, but I knew this now: whoever said that pain healed with time was just making it up for something to say. Pain circled around up high like a bird of prey, and you were a tiny mouse on the ground. At times you didn't even know the bird was up there, but then you might fall under its shadow again. You could either stay in your hole and never go out, or you could run the risk and see what else was outside.

I had my dog and I had my brother's guitar. I had a dad, a sister, and, far away, a gran and a mum. Right now, I suspected, Gabe didn't have anyone.

When we arrived I felt farther away from home than I'd ever been. The jetty rock was cold and silver under the moon. Farther along still, the storm drain groaned and spewed out more water.

There was no way of getting under the bridge tonight because the river was full, much higher now on the steep bank and swamping the place where I'd sat with Gabe. But there was a gap in the orange plastic fencing by the stairs where I could squeeze through and hold it open for Bee. As we went up, Bee brushed against my legs.

This half of the bridge felt truly solid, so I took one step and then another. Up ahead I could see where the concrete had crumbled away, leaving the iron poles that connected one half of the bridge to the other exposed, like an injured limb revealing broken bones. I didn't want to get too close to that. Here would have to do.

I sat down and watched the river twist away in both directions. I took the guitar off my back, and the invisible breeze made me shudder.

Here was Floyd's final song, the final part of the gift he'd left for me: "I Will Follow You into the Dark." I knew this song. Floyd had played it so many times that even Mum, who was his biggest fan, had begged him to learn a new one. I remembered the scene, how she'd held his head against her chest and lovingly told him that she wanted to throttle him sometimes. I remembered the mischief and love in her eyes, and in his.

Oh, I missed her. I mouthed the words into the night as I cried and for once felt not anger but an old, comfortable love.

I hadn't even gotten to the chorus when Gabe appeared, over the other side of the broken bones of the bridge. Quickly I wiped my eyes and remembered what I was here for.

He looked different: less clear, a smudged outline. He was facing the wrong way and the moon shone bright on his shoulders. I stayed silent as my fingers held the vibrations of the strings, and I watched him turn around slowly to his alternate universe.

Eventually his eyes found me.

"Hey," he said. He had a smile in his voice, but he looked less than before. What could that mean about where he was and how I could get there? The sounds of the night creatures were gone and the river lay still. He waved at me, a confused look on his face, perhaps because

I hadn't said a word yet. I didn't want to scare him.

"I went to your house," I said, keeping my voice light. "For real this time."

He looked confused for a moment, but then he remembered. "You did? This is weird. It feels like weeks since I saw you."

"It was only two days ago."

"So... I wasn't there, right? When you came. Because I'd remember that."

I was scared to tell him what his mum had done, how I'd left her, and that he wasn't the one looking after her anymore.

"Something big has happened, Summer." His voice seemed to melt into the space between us, making it hard to hear.

"What? Speak up, Gabe."

He came closer to the gap and instinctively I stepped forward to warn him not to fall. But he's not really here, I told myself.

"Dad came back. Saw how we were living. Like it was some surprise, right? I argued with him as much as I could. Pointed out that I was doing a better job than he could but he said *he* was the adult and *he* was making the decisions. He got Mum some kind of nurse. She's going to *hate* that."

"Oh, Gabe."

"I've let her down."

"No! Never. You loved her in the best way."

So Yana was the nurse, and that was why her things were in Gabe's room. Maybe she took naps there or sometimes stayed over.

Bee was doing a nervous shuffling thing, close to the edge, as if she was desperate to get over to Gabe's side and comfort him.

"So you're living with your dad?"

"He reckons he's taking me on a trip. He's bragging about it. Trip of a lifetime. Yeah, right. I told him I can't leave Mum but he says if I don't take this break and then go back to school after, he'll put Mum in a home. He's all, "It's for the best, son." But I'm only his son when it suits him."

I was only half-listening because an image had just come to me: my brother's hand reaching out to help me up from the ground. I realized that it was from the skateboarding dream last night. But it wasn't me he was helping up, it was Gabe.

"Where does he want to take you?" I gulped. Gabe said he'd never been to London, but he also said he'd never been to the river.

"He won't say. It's a surprise. The real surprise will be him actually following through instead of skipping town again."

A shadow of knowing came over me. We weren't just slipping in and out of each other's place, but time as well.

"But Summer, it's not just that," he continued. "It's that I remember something. I keep having the same dream. I'm looking at the sky through a round window. The sky changes all the time but I don't move. I can see the edges of this window right up close, and it's so beautiful outside but all I get is this perfect circle of a view. I can't leave wherever I am."

He looked at me through a circle he'd made with his hands. "And the round window has lines across it. Five or six maybe. Thin horizontal bars," he said. "Sometimes they flicker and blur."

I clutched the Ibanez Artwood. That's what he was describing. His burrow. His safe place. The bars were the strings; they blurred when I played. Something *had* happened to Gabe, only where he was—*when* he was—it hadn't happened yet. I put my hand to my heart, because it hurt. He'd died in the bomb, hadn't he? That was where this was leading. In his time he hadn't been to London yet, but in mine he had.

"Gabe, what date is it where you are?"

"I think it's . . . twenty-third or twenty-fourth of March."

It wasn't March in my universe. "Which year?"

"2016."

But it wasn't. That was last year. So this was it: somehow he'd met my brother—the skate park dream flashed in front of my eyes like strobe lighting—and somehow they'd ended up at Waterloo Station together. There were still so many holes, but standing between us now was this murky river, half the world, and nearly four hundred days.

"There's that smell again," he said.

"The one from my house?"

"Bleach. And food. Bad food, like school dinners."

So whatever he could smell wasn't in *my* world. School dinners? Was it just a memory?

It was so quiet in our bubble. Nothing I said would be carried away on the wind or drowned in the river. But I had this chance to say good-bye, a chance I hadn't had with Floyd. Was that what this had all been for?

"Gabe, I want you to know that there's nothing to worry about. Everything's going to be okay."

"You sound like you've worked it all out. Have you? I need to come over there where you are."

"No, you can't. You have to stay where you are."

"What do you mean?"

"Just trust me."

"I do, Summer."

"And . . . And I want to tell you something," I said.

241

"What is it?"

What were the right words? I felt something for Gabe that was more than like, but I didn't know what it was. It was some kind of love but it was in a box, wrapped inside many layers, waiting to come out and be love but not yet.

"You were my first friend here," I said.

"Thanks. I'll be back though, Summer."

But he wouldn't. This was torture.

"I know. But still—bye, Gabe."

He was starting to fade. I hugged the guitar, because I couldn't hold him, then held out my hand across the gap in the bridge. When his hand met mine the tips of my fingers sizzled like the ends of sparklers. Then, in a twist of air, he was gone.

I started to sob. I'd been holding it all in—not just this moment, but everything. I cried loudly and messily up there on the bridge, looking over treetops as the brown river rushed again and the wind blew, relentlessly continuing their journeys. I cried for Floyd and Mum. For Gabe. What was it all for? For Mal, for home, for Gran and her sea view, and for Charlotte the cat. For Dad and Wren. And, I can't lie, I cried for me. The old me, who was someone I was supposed to be looking after and had forgotten about. I could never have her back. I had to let her go, too.

Underneath my toes, I felt the edge of the concrete where the bridge ended. I closed my eyes. Now the sound of the river could be anything. It was Gran filling up the watering can while we three played till dusk in her rambling garden. It was a night at the beach, camping with Dad, waves lapping the shore as we fell asleep. It was Mum running me a bath in our tall, crumbling house in London, swishing her hand around too-hot water to make it just right.

I felt Bee right beside me. She barked and ran back along the bridge.

"Bee! Wait!"

A pattering sound began and I noticed that the river water was being speckled with rain. I followed Bee. The rain got heavier; it sounded like a machine and pelted my back with tiny nails, ran down my neck and arms and soaked my hands as one held the metal railing and the other held the guitar. I heard a splash.

"Bee!" I squeezed through the gap in the orange fencing, pulled the guitar through, and looked for her. She was in the river, trying to swim across to the other side, where Gabe had been. But the current was strong, and the rain made it worse. Her head vanished under the water and bobbed up again. "Please, Bee! Come back!"

But she couldn't. She was swept under the bridge and around the corner. I screamed. There was no way down the bank and no path to get downstream to rescue her.

I kept calling her name so she'd know I wasn't going to give up.

"Bee, I'm coming!"

The rain was so loud. I put the guitar down and went to pull off my shoes. The river was fast, and I was terrified, but I loved her so much.

Out of the corner of my eye I saw a movement in the water under the bridge. She had made it! On her long, bandy legs she struggled up the small ledge of bank that was left and I held out my arms to her.

She did a gigantic sneeze and shook herself so her fur stood on end. Then she came into my arms and I hugged her big wet head and kissed her. "I'm sorry, Bee. He's gone. I'm so sorry."

the other side of
chance

I could smell the river on Bee all the way home, and it wasn't good. I didn't know whether to laugh or cry. I kept taking big gulps of air when I thought about Gabe and the fact that he was a kind of ghost after all. And then I'd remember how close I'd come to losing Bee as well. And then I'd get a whiff of her. Oh, Bee.

The rain had stopped. As we turned the corner of our street, I saw a dark figure sitting on the porch bench. Wren had let her hair down and combed out the tangles. It was almost to her waist like Mum's. She had her knees up and she was drawing. When she saw me, she was serious for a moment, but then I saw a faint smile like the one Mum would give me after we'd argued, because she couldn't stay cross with any of us for long.

I walked toward Wren, Bee close by my side, knowing for the first time in ages that I didn't hate my sister, no matter how hard I'd tried to convince myself that I did.

"Hi," I said.

She made a cute expression that I thought meant, well, that's a start.

"Are you going to tell Dad I was out?"

"Doubt it." She sighed. "You'd better go inside and do something about that smell." She smiled faintly, and carried on with her drawing.

I took Bee straight into the downstairs bathroom. In the light I could see she had leaves and twigs in her fur. Mud, as well. I turned on the shower and she stood underneath it. A pure brown river started to collect around her massive paws. We both got completely soaked and she kept shaking off while I was still washing her.

Finally she was clean. As I tried to dry her off a bit, there was a knock on the door.

"Summer? Is that you in there?" said Dad.

"I was just giving Bee a wash." I opened the door. Bee shot out and nearly bowled Dad over. "She rolled in something in the front garden."

Dad looked over my head. The bathroom was in a state. "Geez. Bit of a mess. I'd better mop that floor. Whatever she rolled in is probably riddled with germs."

"I'll do it, Dad."

"Okeydokey. Thanks, sweetheart. I'll get the bleach. I got some powerful stuff the other day. Hospital strength!"

While he went to the kitchen, I had a thought. The smell of bleach. Hospitals. What if Gabe could smell it because that's where he was? What if he wasn't dead, or asleep, but somewhere between the two?

I mopped that floor until it gleamed. I was right. *I was right*. The amazing Ibanez Artwood wasn't meant to stop time or change time, and it wasn't just giving me another person to say good-bye to. It was a message and finally it had been delivered: Find Gabe. He's alive.

—*Did you work it out, Summer?*

You knew all along. You knew him.

—*I'm just here to look out for you. No one wants their big brother running the show.*

I miss you, Floyd.

—*I know. I love you, Summer.*

I love you, too.

I went to bed that night wondering where I would go in my sleep and where I would be when I woke.

The pillow has a strange smell. I lift my face a bit, and something rough on my cheek scratches against the fabric.

The door slams, and instantly I'm wide-awake and on my guard.

Dad's home.

I get out of bed and stand behind the door. Noises in the hallway; Dad is ramming into the wall at random intervals, getting closer. *He's been drinking. Again.*

I hear his voice, mumbling and growling. *He's always like this after the fun has worn off.* I wrap my arms around myself and it almost feels like someone else is holding me. I sense Dad's body press against the door, and then he slurs, "Should've left him at home with his crazy mother." I want to open the door and punch his stupid face. The feeling that I should never have come here gnaws at me. *He made me leave Mum. I need to get home.*

Time catches on a nail, and when it breaks off again it's daylight.

"Gabe? You up?"

There's a faraway knocking. The door looks like it's at the end of a long tunnel. The knocking gets closer and louder.

"Gabe! Someone here to see you."

Floyd's here.

I flip my board off the ground and into my hand. I'm dressed and ready. Floyd holds up two guitars. "More lessons. Come on. Let's get out of here."

We're walking along a street, narrow with tall houses. *You've been skating and busking all day. It's been the best. You're going to miss him when you go back to Mum.*

Floyd's talking, describing his family. "Mum's a bit of a hippy. An artist. Watch out for her bear hugs—she could break a rib no problem." *She's the one he adores.*

"Dad rubs me the wrong way. Can't help himself. Wren could melt you with her death stare, but she's got a heart of gold. It's just that it's locked in a secret crypt and guarded by rabid monkeys. And then there's Summer. She's funny and smart but doesn't know it yet."

We walk into a house. Floyd's still talking, but I'm only half-listening. I'm staring at every single thing and taking in the sounds. I shake hands with his mum and his dad, get a glare from his sister, and decide I like them already.

We eat dinner and it's as if an hour has slipped through my fingers like water. Floyd disappears down some steps that go belowground and comes back up with a skate ramp that looks homemade.

"Don't scrape the wall with that!" his dad shouts at the exact moment I hear the wood make contact.

"Run before he catches up," Floyd whispers.

I touch the long scar on the wall and flinch before following him outside to the street.

It's dark. I'm in Floyd's room. He's playing an old guitar and I'm playing his beautiful one. Wren's here, singing. We sound good, I think. I want to stay like this. I don't want the song to end.

Floyd's sleeping on the floor next to his bed. He faces away from me and I watch his shoulder rise and fall. *You'll miss him.* Two guitars lean like twin brothers against the wall. *You wish your mum could be here. You think she'd like these people.*

Just for tonight, you let yourself feel like part of the family.

the other side of cyberspace

I woke in Dad's bed the next morning. He was already up. I wondered if he was going to ask me about sleep-walking, or let it go. As I stretched and yawned and remembered Dad's warm-bread smell, my mind was losing the dream I'd just had as if it were water slipping down a drain. I grabbed droplets of it: I'd been at home, playing the Ibanez Artwood with my brother. No, with my *friend*, Floyd, because in the dream I'd been Gabe.

When I came out of Dad's room there was an ear-splitting noise. Dad was in the back garden attacking the hedge with the set of angry sawfish teeth he was always borrowing from Mike Witkin. It filled the house with an unfriendly grinding, like nails in a blender.

But then I heard something else, faint and delicate like music from a music box. I followed the noise and saw Dad's laptop on the kitchen table with the Skype window open.

Mum was calling.

I shouted for Dad, but he must have had safety earmuffs on—either that or he couldn't hear over the noise he was making. I'd have to ignore it. I wanted Mum back, but I wasn't ready. Mesmerized by the screen, heart beating too hard, I walked toward the kitchen bench and started to make toast.

She hung up; I breathed out.

The grinding metal sound from the garden was loud enough to bury my thoughts. I got the peanut butter, a plate, and a knife and stood over the toaster.

Beep-boop-beep: the gentle calling started up again.

"Wren! Dad!" I shouted, partly to be heard over the noise but partly because I was angry at them for leaving me alone when something like this might happen.

No answer.

She hung up. She rang again. She hung up. The sound seemed more impatient every time. By the time the toast popped up I'd lost my appetite.

I sat down in front of the laptop. If it rings once more, I told myself, I'll answer it.

Beep-boop-beep. Beep-boop-beep. Beep-boop-beep.

One click of the green handset.

"Hello! You're there!" At first Mum was just a voice; she hadn't turned on the video camera yet and neither had I. She didn't know it was me; she thought she was talking to Dad or Wren. There was still time to back down.

"Can you hear me?" she said. "I can't hear you!" I could tell she was clicking the mouse with increasing frustration. "I always have trouble with this thing." It was so familiar, picturing Mum fighting with a piece of technology. She could never work her phone, either; she was always more comfortable with a paintbrush in her hand.

I felt like I was going to cry before we'd even started talking. Her voice and these random memories of her slotted into my heart like the missing puzzle piece that's been stuck to the bottom of your bare foot all along. And it was her old voice, too, not the whisper-quiet one. The sound reached deeply into a place that I'd tried to forget.

"It's me, Mum," I said.

The screen flickered, and a glow that was black and gold like a burning photograph became my mum's face in front of one of the small square kitchen windows in Gran's house. A low sun blinking behind her; green fields just visible in the distance.

Home. Mum and home. It was a shock, like looking into a mirror after a really long time when you'd almost forgotten what you looked like, who you were.

"Summer? Why can't I see you?" she said, panicking. I saw her hand reach out to the screen. Her lip was quivering.

I turned on the video camera.

"Oh. Oh, there you are," she said, sobbing. "Oh God, sorry." She wiped her eyes roughly. "Please don't go. I'm so happy to see you, Summer." She cried through her smile, and I realized that my face was completely soaked in tears.

"Hi, Mum," I said in a tiny voice.

"Hi, sweetheart."

It was hard to believe she wasn't in the same room as me. She looked thinner in her face and shadowy under her eyes but still so much better than the last time I saw her. She had color in her cheeks and had done her hair the way she used to, piled loosely on her head so that it looked like it might fall over at any moment. She was wearing the necklace of big wooden orange beads that I'd bought her one Christmas, which she'd said reminded her of the tiny mandarins Gran used to put in her stocking.

We didn't know what to say. For a while we just gazed at each other and it was unreal. We both giggled nervously a few times. Then Mum took charge and started asking me questions about Australia and school and the neighbors and new friends. Immediately I felt my stomach muscles tighten. I didn't want her to ask that sort of thing yet. It only reminded me that she hadn't been part of my life. And that I was hurt.

I needed to trust her again, and I thought I knew a way I might be able to. What if she could help me find Gabe? But I was scared. It was so hard to ask Mum for anything, let alone something that might make her think I was crazy.

"Mum, I need you. Please listen to me until I've told you everything. It's about Floyd's friend Gabe."

I spoke slowly and carefully because I needed to tell her what I knew but not how I knew it, and I didn't want to trip up. I mixed up lies with truth; I told Mum a story that she could believe.

"And that's it. He needs my help."

"Why are you so sure that Gabriel's hurt somewhere and no one's looking after him? They would have notified his family."

"But they didn't. I just know, Mum. I'm sure he's in a hospital over there. And I think he needs help. He's . . . He's trapped in a place where he doesn't belong."

Before I could say anything more to convince her, Dad slid open the door, panting and shining with sweat, and, as if I'd been caught doing something wrong, I slammed the laptop shut.

the other side of
Wren

Later I went out front to sit on my porch bench. But Wren was already there, drawing again. I was about to go back in when she patted the seat beside her without even looking up. I sat down and watched Wren's face as she drew. Her eyes were dark and intense and her mouth twitched, as if to show the decisions she was making as she worked.

When I looked at her sketchpad, I gasped.

"What's wrong?" she said.

I pointed to a charcoal face, with its breathtaking detail and the smudge of white chalk across one eye.

"You know him?" I asked.

She frowned and looked at the pad. "Summer, it's Floyd. Don't you think it looks like him?"

"Not Floyd. The other face."

She held the drawing to her chest. "Don't get upset. It's just a drawing."

"What do you mean? What do you know about him? Why are you drawing him?"

"Summer, don't yell." Her voice cracked. Her eyes filled with tears.

"He is real, isn't he?" I asked. I knew my face was a mirror image of hers, crumpled and sad.

"Of course!" she said in a high-pitched whisper. "Of course he's real. I met him, but only once. I just can't stop drawing the two of them. I've been doing the same drawings every day lately." Suddenly her eyes were strong and wide, a warning, a flash of fire. "Don't tell Dad. He'll just worry about me."

"I promise I won't."

"But how did you know him?" she said. "He came to our house, but you weren't there."

"I know him from somewhere else."

I don't think she believed me, but she carried on.

"No one ever talked about it because it was Floyd's last night. We were writing a song in Floyd's room. After dinner."

"All three of you?"

"They just needed someone to sing some harmonies."

"I didn't even know you liked singing." I thought of

Floyd teaching me guitar and how I'd always thought that music was a thing for him and me and no one else.

"We had different times together, Summer. Me and Floyd were actually good mates, even if it looked like we were fighting a lot of the time."

All this time I'd had Floyd in my head, thinking he was mine to hang on to. But he was Wren's, too.

"What was he like? Floyd's friend, I mean."

"The strange thing is, I can't even remember his name, but I remember the feeling of him in the room. That sounds weird, right?"

"No, it doesn't."

"He had a kind of . . . presence. He seemed older than fifteen. Kind of wise. And solid. Like there was a lot going on inside. Floyd said they hadn't known each other long, but they felt like brothers."

"What else?"

"Why?"

"Please, Wren. I missed that night."

"All right. Well, I remember they went skateboarding after dinner. And Dad was cranky because—"

"Stop. I know this. Was it because they marked the wall? In the hallway by the cellar?"

"That's it. And he was really polite. Good-looking. Had an Aussie accent . . . Hey, I'd forgotten that bit until now. Oh, and Floyd had only been teaching him guitar for a couple of weeks but he was already amazing. I think Floyd was a bit jealous, but you could tell he was fighting it because he liked this guy so much."

"They met in a skate park."

"Oh, so Floyd did tell you about him?"

"Yes. Sort of."

"Summer, you're being kind of weird. Are you okay?"

"I will be." I put my arms around Wren and leaned closer until my face was covered in the forest of her magnificent hair. She smelled of lavender and moonlight.

———

When Dad and Wren went to sleep that night, I tried to bring Gabe back with the Ibanez Artwood. I wanted to speak to him, to see him, to tell him I was still looking. I didn't care if he appeared in the garden or my bedroom or on the roof, as long as he came. But every time I thought he'd appeared, it was just a shadow moving on my wall, or a breath of air through the window. It wasn't working anymore.

This must have been what it was like for Mal, I thought. I'd disappeared out of her life, just like that. Gabe and Mal were now both holes in mine. So, that night before I went to sleep, I wrote down more of my story for her.

———

The indoor skate park is heaving. We've just finished an intense session and now we're sitting to the side on our boards, passing a drink between us. I hand the bottle back empty to Floyd and wait for him to elbow me. He does, and when I laugh the lemonade in my mouth spills down my chin. And then *he* laughs.

This is where we first met. We're underneath Waterloo Station. Soon we'll head up there to the trains and I can't believe it's nearly time to say goodbye. *You're going home.*

I feel the adrenaline of the last few weeks in every muscle. The whole place seems electrified, and I feel like the source. *You've come to the other side of the world. You've met Floyd, who feels like a brother. You never had a brother or a sister before, just Mum.*

"Check this out." I hand a piece of paper to Floyd.

"Is this what he left you? 'This will be good for you.' Unbelievable."

It's the note from Dad. He packed up and left in the night. He always leaves you first, even when you're planning on leaving him.

"Will you be all right, G?"

"Yeah, I'm good. This break has made me feel a lot better about looking after Mum. I can do it."

"I'll come visit you as soon as I can. Dad's always said we'll go to Oz one day."

"Cool. That'd be awesome."

We bump fists without looking at each other. *You wish your worlds weren't so far apart.*

Floyd stretches out his arm and grabs the Ibanez Artwood. He hands it to you and grabs his spare.

"Final jam?"

"Here?"

"Yeah, here."

I see Floyd smiling shyly at someone sitting farther along the wall. *It's a girl you were skating with. She knows more tricks than the two of you put together.*

I chuckle discreetly, into my chest, because it looks like the usually cool Floyd is in love. I lean forward and see that she has the exact same look on her face.

I play some chords very lightly, making sure I'm in tune. This guitar is beautiful. The sound is like nature and magic.

Floyd made you borrow the Ibanez Artwood for the last few weeks, even though you didn't want to at first because you were so worried you'd scratch it. You're going to miss this, too. Floyd has been playing his old one, which he says you can take back home with you. He said, "Don't tell my sister. We're buying her a new one for her thirteenth, anyway."

Floyd starts to play "Waterloo Sunset" by The Kinks. He's note perfect. I want to be as good as he is one day. I try to play it too, singing the worst sha-la-las anyone's ever heard and all the bits about Waterloo sunset being fine. I sense bodies gathering near us to listen, but I don't look up or I'll lose my nerve. This is a moment I'll never forget.

Floyd's girl is gazing at him. They're smiling like they have a secret.

When I flick the final note of the song, time flicks too. I'm standing in the station. The guitar is still in my hands; the Ibanez Artwood. Floyd is walking away from me with the girl and his other guitar, the spare, the one he was going to give me. They're heading toward the clock and I realize I've missed something. We've already said good-bye. It's over. But then, why am I still holding the Ibanez Artwood? This can't be right. He'd never give this up. He loves this guitar.

I can still see them, winding their way through the crowds. I'm not sure if I've thanked him enough for the last few weeks. For everything. Has he really given me this guitar?

"Floyd!" I yell, at the top of my voice. "Hey, brother!"

He turns around, and even from far away I can feel his smile. I hold up the Ibanez Artwood, and he holds up one hand: it's yours.

the other side of
a hiding place

When I woke, I felt like every particle of the dream was in my bloodstream. I counted back the hours to see what time it would be back home. The house was quiet, and I crept downstairs to the kitchen table, where the laptop was always plugged in.

I don't know how long I stared at the screen. I was wiggling my fingers lightly, trying to keep the pictures from my dream circulating and at the same time working up courage. I couldn't put into words what I was scared of.

—*Call her, Sum.*

She might not want me to.

—*You know she does. You know Mum.*

Not like I used to.

—The old Mum is still there. Just like the old Summer.

So the old Summer tried to call the old Mum, and Floyd was right. It was awkward at first, but suddenly Gran appeared in the background and leaned over Mum's shoulder.

"How's my Summer?" she said gruffly and affectionately like only Gran could.

"She's all right, Gran. How are you? And how's Charlotte?"

"That dreadful cat keeps leaving dead mice in my slippers." She suddenly straightened up so I couldn't see her head anymore. "I'm off to get some wood now. Be good!" And as Mum and I laughed, I think we both relaxed.

Mum had been searching for Gabe like I asked. She'd called forty-eight out of sixty London hospitals, and not one of them had admitted a boy called Gabriel de Souza in the past year. She'd been to the local police station, too, but they'd been no help. They couldn't search for an allegedly missing person who wasn't even related to us. And she couldn't even tell them his dad's name, because de Souza was his mum's and I'd never thought to ask.

Mum had also gone through every piece of news about the bomb. When she told me that, I started to cry.

I was terrified of what this might be doing to her, but she held her hand out to the screen and said that she was doing well and that she wished she could hold me.

"I can't look away from what happened to our boy, can I?" she said.

Then we both cried, and it didn't feel 100 percent like sadness.

The next time, Mum called me. But the news wasn't any better. She'd called all sixty hospitals. There was nowhere else to try.

"It's not adding up," said Mum. "Maybe you've got your story wrong, darling. Didn't you say that Gabriel had been traveling with his father? They could have gone anywhere. He's probably perfectly well, walking around Rome or Paris, seeing the world with his dad."

"He's not! I know he's not."

"*How*, Summer?"

"I just do. And I promised him! You promised *me*!"

All of a sudden the rage was there again. Mum tried to reach out to me with her hand as if she could touch me through the screen, but all she managed to do was block the camera so that everything went black. This time it didn't seem cute or funny; it made me angry. I couldn't stop myself. I slammed the laptop shut before her face could reappear. I regretted it as soon as I'd done it, but that just made the anger grow hotter.

I spent hours on the internet researching how to find missing people. There were more than eight million people in London and more than sixty-four million people in the UK. Searching for Gabe was like looking for a particular grain of sand on the beach. But that didn't mean the grain of sand wasn't there, did it?

Even though every day I felt like giving up, the thought that I was responsible for another person stopped me from curling up in a cocoon again.

The next dream I had made me do something the minute I woke up. Because for the second time I remembered every detail of it.

———

Beep. Beep. Beep.

I'm in a bed. My eyes are closed and too heavy to open. I hear a voice. "Check the monitor." And then another. "Pulse good, blood pressure good, temperature spike last night, but it's come down now. He's doing well, doctor." A pause, then a different voice. "Yes, it's true that he's recovered well from the internal injuries. But the longer the coma continues..."

The voices fade and I think that the people they belong to are leaving the room. All I can hear are the beeps. I picture the lines on the monitor I must be attached to.

The dream skips like someone nudging the needle on a record player. Now my eyes are open and everything's bright. I'm not in a bed, I'm inside a room that smells sweet like wood. It's dark and small and there's a perfectly circular window. There are lines across it, like bars. Are they what's keeping me inside?

The bars suddenly move up and down. They vibrate and the room is filled with sound. These aren't bars, they're strings. This is my life support. And I need to come off it now.

———

I woke in the garden, curled up on the grass with the guitar. I knew what I had to do. Leaving the guitar there, I went inside and found Wren's art supplies that she kept in an old wooden toolbox. The house was quiet apart from the sound of me rummaging and the clock on the kitchen wall ticking. It was two o'clock in the morning. Breathing hard, scared that I'd lose my courage, I finally found her large metal scissors. Back outside, I knelt down next to the Ibanez Artwood. Under the moonlight I guided the scissors around the first string and pressed the blades together with both hands, using all my strength. *Snap!* And the next string. *Snap!* I cut them all, one by one.

the other side of the Street

I felt numb about what I'd done to the guitar because I'd expected something instant and magical to happen. I thought I'd set Gabe free, but what did that mean? There was no sign that I'd done anything apart from ruin my brother's most precious possession. Life—*my* life, anyway—was the same as usual.

Although that wasn't completely true. One thing was better. Wren and I were side by side on the porch bench again, with Bee at our feet. This was becoming our place.

Earlier, she'd let me borrow a pair of her black jeans and she'd braided my hair.

"Hey, you've grown," she'd said when I was trying on her stuff.

"Have I?" I hadn't believed it, even though my feet poking out of the legs of her jeans said that it must be true.

Now we were watching Milo shoot hoops. We cheered loudly whenever he got one in. He pretended not to enjoy it, but I could tell he did. He still wasn't very good, so Wren and I had plenty of time to talk in between.

"Wren," I started, not really sure if I should continue. "When did you . . . Why did you . . . No, *how* did you suddenly become so nice?" I looked at her nervously and then smiled clownishly, hoping she'd know I meant it in a nice way.

"I'm not nice!" she said.

I raised an eyebrow.

"Fine. Look, I just decided. After what Gran said. I decided I would *pretend* to be nice to you and Dad."

I started to giggle and then she did, too.

"And after a while, it wasn't so difficult. I got used to it. Also, when no one's looking I pull wings off butterflies."

"I knew it."

We watched Milo again.

"Have you kissed him?" I said after a while.

"Sh!" Wren nudged me.

"Ow! Well, have you?"

"Not yet. I'm not sure if I want to."

"How come?"

She shrugged. "I'm not sure if I like boys that way. I mean, I do, but I also like girls. And not everyone is going to be okay with that. So . . ."

I looked at Milo and tried to act cool. My sister had never shared anything like that with me, and I didn't want to get this wrong.

"I think he'd be okay with it. He's Milo. He's pretty awesome. And he *should* be okay with it. Everyone should be."

"I know they should. I feel like they should. But thanks. Ratbag." She nudged me again, and this time she smiled so widely that her dimple showed.

I'd forgotten she had one. I didn't say anything, but I smiled back and felt six feet tall.

We sat there for a while, then Milo got two in a row so we got on our feet, cheering. That's when I saw her. The woman was at the top of the street, in front of a yellow taxi. Clue number one: the woman had a suitcase. Clue number two: her hair was down to her waist.

Wren was still cheering, and I tugged her sleeve. Clue number three: Wren froze too. She'd seen. I watched her trying to believe her eyes like I was.

Wren and I stepped off the porch together. I was still holding Wren's sleeve.

Clue number four: the woman was walking toward us, fast, faster.

Clue number five: Wren opened the gate and started to run. I ran too. I caught up with her and when Wren glanced at me (clue number six) she had tears in her eyes and was smiling.

We got there at the same time. The woman held out her arms.

Clue number seven: her smell. Clue number eight: how tightly she held me. Clue number nine: the way I cried and cried and cried.

Clue number ten: I looked up at Mum's face and she smiled.

the other side of
a question

On Saturday morning there was a knock on my bedroom door. It was Mum. My heart still jumped whenever I saw her.

"Can I come in?"

I propped myself up on my elbow and patted the end of my bed.

"I've had an idea. I know you said Gabriel's mother was ill with dementia, but we should go back to see her, don't you think? Maybe we'll discover something."

I nodded, overwhelmed that Mum was still thinking about this. Since she'd arrived, three days ago, Mum had been asleep a lot because of jet lag and we'd hardly been alone.

273

"I can't seem to rest easy without knowing what happened," she said. "And if Gabriel was the last person to see Floyd . . . Well, I'd just like to talk to him. I'm still wondering if he's just traveling with his dad," she said. "And there's us ringing hospitals . . . Gabriel's probably having the time of his life."

"It's "Gabe," Mum, and I already told you he's not." I didn't mean to snap, and part of me worried that she'd get up and walk out and go straight back home if I was rude or mean. But all she did was look into my eyes, deeply, and touch my face.

"Come on, then. Up you get and we'll see what we can find out."

I took Mum to Gabe's building the long way, along the beautiful creek. On the way we talked about all the little details of my life that were new to her. It made me realize that so much had become familiar to me and I hadn't even noticed. I wasn't so much a stranger here as I had been.

When we got there, I pointed up toward the windows of Gabe's apartment.

"Please tell me there's an elevator," said Mum.

From the hallway at the top level we could see right into Gabe's kitchen, but it didn't look like anyone was there. Mum rang the doorbell. The woman who answered was very tall, like the one I'd seen that night and thought must be Yana. She didn't look happy about being disturbed.

"Yes?"

"Hello, I'm Cece and this is my daughter Summer. Um . . . This is a bit complicated, but I believe my son knew a boy who used to live here."

"A boy? What boy?"

"We're looking for Gabriel," said Mum.

The woman looked suspiciously from me to Mum. She didn't look like she was going to say a word in reply, and Mum looked at me as if to say, "What now?"

"Are you Yana?" I said shyly.

She narrowed her eyes and looked down her nose at me. I tried hard to keep going, feeling my way around each of my words because although they'd be true, they wouldn't be the *whole* truth. "Gabe was my brother's friend. They were very close. And, well, my brother died and I promised that I'd find Gabe and make sure he was okay. Do you know anything about where he is?"

Her expression changed almost imperceptibly, but enough to let me know she wasn't a mean person, she was just being careful. "I don't know everything. I am just Mrs. de Souza's caregiver. And Mrs. de Souza is not well enough, you understand?"

I nodded. Yana's accent had made her sound cross at the start, but that same accent now sounded kind.

"He was in an accident. Many injuries."

I felt Mum's hand tighten on my shoulder. "But he's not dead," I said.

"Not dead," she said sternly, as if she meant "only just," but all I cared about was that Gabe was really alive, just like he'd told me.

"When you say 'accident,'" said Mum, "what do you mean?" Her voice sounded shaky, and I wondered again if I'd done the wrong thing in asking Mum for help.

"He was in a bad car crash. He is at the Royal Melbourne, that's all I know."

The word "Melbourne" rang in my ears as if Yana had crashed cymbals together right next to my head. He was here all along.

"Mrs. de Souza doesn't visit," said Yana. "It's not good for her. She knows him one day, doesn't know him the next." Yana looked over her shoulder. "It's been a long time." She shook her head solemnly.

Then everything around me seemed to go quiet, like I was in our bubble again, as what Yana said sank in. I stared at her without really seeing her. I knew that Mum had put her arm around me, but I couldn't really feel it.

Gabe was here in Melbourne.

the other side of waking

"We have to go there. Now!" I was striding ahead, without any idea of the direction we should be going.

"Summer, breathe. Remember what that woman said. Gabriel has been hit by a car and he's been in a coma for weeks."

"But how did he . . . ? But why . . . ?" I was thinking about the guitar and the snatches of my dreams that kept flying at me like tiny swooping birds but never stayed in one place long enough for me to see them properly.

"I'm worried you're getting your hopes up," said Mum, stopping me finally.

I was surprised to find she was right. I still had hope. "I can't help it."

Mum's eyes were sparkling, and then hesitantly she put her arms around me. "You've grown up a lot. I'm so sorry, Summer."

I stopped for a moment and looked at Mum properly. I didn't say it was okay, but I did squeeze her tight.

———

Mum had obviously been doing some private plotting on our way to the hospital because when we eventually found the right ward she told the nurse on the desk that we were Gabe's second cousins from England. I wasn't even sure what a second cousin was.

"Well, you've come a long way!" he said, smiling. When he stood up he seemed to go on forever; he was at least six foot five, with a shiny bald head. His badge said Nasib. He called to another nurse and asked her to look after the desk.

"These people have come to see Gabriel," he told her.

It sunk in deeper that he was really here.

Nasib started walking briskly in silent shoes, and I wanted to tell him to slow down, I wasn't ready. But it was happening. I had to let myself get carried along, though my legs were jelly.

"We were wondering if anyone was going to show up for the poor boy," said Nasib, glancing back. He was holding a clipboard close to his chest. I wondered if it held Gabe's medical notes, and what they would say. We passed room after room of patients, turned into another corridor, kept walking.

"The surgeon will come and speak to you properly. Gabriel came out of his coma a few days ago and we've been working on various things since then."

"What date? What time?" I said.

Nasib stopped and checked his chart. "Two a.m., Wednesday. Why, is that significant?"

"No, I mean, I just wondered." I knew it. That was when I'd cut the guitar strings. I hadn't been able to look at the Ibanez Artwood since then. But the magic had happened.

"He's had an operation today—a big one—so we're hoping he's going to wake soon and we can see if we've fixed the damage. It'll be wonderful for him to see familiar faces."

Mum smiled and gave me a worried look. She took my hand.

Nasib stopped by a doorway, blocking it with his enormous frame. We were finally here. "Don't expect miracles," he said. "But we're hopeful. He had some pretty strange injuries for a car accident—especially as the driver of the car claimed they weren't going very fast—but we think he's come out of the worst of it now."

"Well, you see, I don't think he was *just* in a car accident," I said, pulling on Mum's hand because she was trying to make me go in before I was ready. "I think Gabe was injured before the car accident. By a bomb in London, just before he got back here."

"A bomb? That's quite some claim. How do you know this?"

I bit my bottom lip. "I don't know for sure."

"Well, I'm not sure what to say. Surely someone couldn't be so unlucky? Then again, I've seen some things in this job that most people wouldn't believe."

Nasib was being kind. I knew he was suspicious of what I was saying, but then he looked at his notes and I saw from his expression that what I was telling him made a bit of sense. He swung his body like a door opening to show us we'd arrived.

"I'll be back in a moment," he said.

Gabe. It was really Gabe. The sight of him squeezed my heart painfully. His head was bandaged but the top of his scalp was showing. They'd shaved all his hair off. He looked peaceful. And so real. The way he'd looked to me before, in our bubble, seemed like a hologram compared to how he looked now. His skin was darker, his edges were more defined. I was so scared. He might not know me. Or he might know me but it might not feel the same. He could wake and be free of our bubble, but I'd stay trapped inside it, wanting things to be the way they were.

We sat by the side of his bed. Mum held his hand. I knew she'd be thinking about Floyd.

—I'm here, Summer.

I know you are. Thank you. This is so hard, Floyd. I wish you were . . .

—I know.

Once or twice I thought I saw Gabe's eyelashes flicker, and I held my breath, but in the next moment he seemed to be sleeping as deeply as before.

A while later, Nasib came back in.

"Right. Looks like someone's having a sleep-in," he said sternly but with a hint of affection for Gabe, like he was Gabe's big brother. "Come on, sleepyhead. Rise and shine." He leaned over me and shook Gabe's arm gently but firmly.

Gabe turned his head toward us, and I think all three of us gasped.

"I think it's happening, ladies," said Nasib.

A tiny frown appeared on Gabe's forehead. His arm muscles twitched. He flexed his fingers. His eyes opened and he looked at Nasib.

"Welcome back, Mr. de Souza," said Nasib warmly. As he stepped back and made a note on his chart, Gabe looked at me. His eyes suddenly burst wider and his face was exactly like the time I'd first spoken to him in my bedroom, full of fear and shock. He started breathing heavily.

"What's happening? Where am I? Summer! Who are these people?" He was grabbing at wires that were attached to him and trying in vain to raise his head.

Nasib stepped between us to try to make him lie down, and I had to walk around to the end of the bed so I could see Gabe and let him see me.

"Gabriel, you're okay, but you must lie still and relax," Nasib said firmly.

"Who are you?" he said. He tried to shout but his voice was rasping.

"You know me, Gabriel. I'm Nasib. I've been looking after you."

Gabe tried to get up again. "Summer, what is this place? Summer! Help me!"

"Gabe! It's okay!" I cupped my hands over my mouth and cried.

Gabe was thrashing around, but he was much too weak, and Nasib held him down easily.

"How does he know you, Summer?" whispered Mum, coming to my side again.

Gabe's eyes were closing again.

"Is he okay? Why's he closing his eyes?" I yelled at Nasib.

"He'll be fine. I've seen this many times. More often in younger children, though." Nasib checked the bag attached to the drip going into Gabe's arm, and then gently rested his hand on Gabe's forehead. "It's called emergence delirium. Patients wake up and have no memory of why they're here. Often they don't even know their own family, so at least it's something that he recognized you, eh?" He smiled at me, and then returned to check Gabe's pulse and heartbeat. "He'll wake up again in a moment, and he'll be calm and remember why he's here."

I counted the seconds. Exactly four minutes and twenty-five seconds after he'd first woken, Gabe woke again. He looked at the nurse.

"Nas," he said.

Nasib lay one of his giant hands on Gabe's arm. "That's more like it. Now, do you know these people?"

Gabe's head turned to my mum. He frowned, blinked slowly.

"Floyd's mum," he said.

"That's right," Mum said softly. She had tears in her eyes.

"I don't understand." He coughed and looked at the nurse, who seemed to know that what he needed was water. He held a straw to Gabe's lips.

"Your cousins have come to see you," said Nasib.

"Cousins?"

Nasib gave Mum a gently scolding look. "Mmm . . . Well, close friends, perhaps? You know this lovely girl here, though, remember?" Nasib beckoned me closer. "Come on, Gabriel, you just said her name not five minutes ago."

I could see Gabe searching his mind, not finding me, and I had to look away.

"Well, not to worry, now. It'll come to you." Nasib's warm, happy voice was such a strange birdsong in this room. He wheeled a machine around the back of me and out of the room. "Shall we go and have a quick chat about things?" he said to Mum.

"Will you be all right for a moment, Summer?" said Mum.

I nodded. Mum looked a mixture of teary and suspicious as she left me. I couldn't blame her. But I knew we trusted each other in the most important way.

And then once again it was like the time Gabe had appeared in my bedroom, when I'd had to count to three and then turn around and look him directly in the eyes.

"Summer?" said Gabe.

I nodded, my heart catching.

"And we've met?"

So this was how it was going to be. He didn't

284

remember me with the part of his brain that did most of the thinking. I was buried somewhere else.

"Not properly." I smiled awkwardly. There were things I needed to know, and questions he'd have, too, eventually. But it didn't matter whether Gabe remembered me now, in the next hour, or ever. Because we were here in the same place, at the same time, and that was a wish or a miracle, whichever way I looked at it.

part three

ONE AND A HALF
YEARS LATER

the other side of Christmas

It wasn't like the Christmases I remembered from when I was little. For a start, what woke me up was a combination of the sun blazing through my window like a hot iron on the side of my face, and Dad cranking up the lawnmower.

"Perfect! Merry Christmas!" shouted Wren in a mocking voice from across the hallway.

I giggled and shifted into the shady part of my bed. "Merry Christmas to you too!" I yelled back. Bee was stretched out in the patch of sun on my bed, snoring, and I gently held one of her huge paws.

My phone bleeped twice and I reached for it without getting up. It was a Merry Christmas message from

Becky, who was spending the summer holidays in Perth with her family. She'd used every single Christmas and celebration emoji she could find, and finished with a prawn. Typical of lovely, funny Becky.

I heard pitter-patters, and Wren appeared in the doorway, all thick, wild hair and smudged eye makeup. She wore an Emily the Strange T-shirt that said "Get Lost," but she smiled with her whole face.

"Well? What did you get?" she said.

"What?"

"In your stocking!" She brought hers from behind her back and pointed to the end of my bed.

"I didn't know we were getting stockings again. We haven't had them since you told me Father Christmas wasn't real and Mum decided there was no point."

"You needed to know the truth."

"You told me I wasn't real, either, and that everyone was just pretending to see me."

"Wow, Old Wren was funny. Anyway, you're real, aren't you? Ergo Father Christmas is real, too. Except here he's called Santa."

I raised one eyebrow and patted a space for her to sit down.

I was nervous about today. Christmas had been packed away in a box for two years. The first year, we couldn't even open the lid because of Floyd. The year after that we would have tried had the Shadow not visited Mum. Although that second year we'd flown back home for a Christmas we could recognize—*cold*, I mean—London had just been a signpost on the motorway that we'd passed by on our way to Gran's. We'd holed up in Cornwall for two weeks, ignoring everything festive apart from eating a lot. That part wasn't, and still isn't, optional at Gran's. But this year she'd decided to go on a cruise. And I was ready to see what Christmas was like in our new home.

Some people called Mum's Shadow a black dog, a demon, or a dark place. The way I saw it, it was like a tall cloaked figure that would creep up on Mum and wrap her up so tightly that she couldn't move or even look up to see our faces.

The Shadow meant depression. Sometimes it was better to call it that instead. It came and went. Mum had pills for it and mostly they worked. We still didn't know how to carry on without Mum in the times she wasn't quite with us, but we were getting better at it.

She was with us today, though, in all the ways she could be.

This December, the Christmas box had been opened, and we'd dug deep inside. I worried that the lights would be too tangled to be unraveled, or that all the shiny baubles might have cracked like eggshells, showing us that whatever Christmas magic had once been inside them was long gone. But then I told myself that this Christmas didn't have to be exactly like old times to be a happy one. Just as long as there were a few old things to remind us.

Chocolate coins, for one. Wren and I ripped open a big net of giant ones. Dad had called a temporary ceasefire in his war against junk food. We teased open the foil of the biggest coins and shoved them in our mouths; then we rummaged around the things we'd tipped onto my bed.

"New eyeliner. Thanks, Mum," said Wren, with the chocolate going all gooey in her teeth.

I looked at my little gifts one by one: a beautiful leather pick holder, a new guitar strap, a book, a three-pack of lip balm, and something that looked a bit like a coat hook.

"What's this?" I asked Wren.

"Oh, I know! Remember Floyd had one? You screw it into the wall and you can hang your guitar on it. Or your little sister . . ." She looked guiltily out of the window, smirking, and a memory came to me of Wren and Floyd hooking the label of my jumper over the guitar hanger so that when I tried to walk away I was trapped. I slapped her leg and took one of her chocolate coins.

"Wait, there's one more thing," I said, digging deeper into the stocking. "A mandarin!" We giggled. "Of course. Dad has to make sure we get our five a day."

Wren made a mandarin sandwich with a chocolate coin as the filling, and popped it into her mouth whole. "So. Excited about who's coming later?" she said with her mouth full.

"Sure," I said in a small voice.

She kicked me and smiled, and just then Mike Witkin's hedge trimmer started up.

"Excellent!" yelled Wren. "So festive!" We laughed again, and rolled around on my sunlit bed like a pair of happy cats.

the other side of
us

Downstairs, Dad had gone completely overboard. There were flashy decorations inside and out. We had a seven-foot tree inside, and he'd put a huge blow-up reindeer in the front garden. Its nose glowed.

In the old days, Mum would have banned the whole lot. She'd never liked the tacky side of holidays, only the stories and the symbolism and the way it brought families together. She'd gather winter twigs into vases and hang dried orange slices and cinnamon sticks on their branches; she'd string fresh holly and mistletoe all around the house, and if anyone suggested fake snow on the windows she'd only have to give them a look.

But this year Mum must have been able to see that Dad had never been more at home. This was a Christmas that made sense to him. He'd been preparing food since last week. Opening the fridge was risky because there was so much crammed in there that taking out any item was like playing Jenga. Dad had been wearing a Santa hat for three days solid. He'd probably been sleeping in it. It got worse: he was making Bee wear one too. But she put up with it, so maybe we all could.

It was only if you looked really closely and at exactly the right moment that you would ever see a flicker of sadness on Dad's face. I knew it happened at the times he wished Floyd was here, joining in, behaving like a Christmas fool. But Dad never liked to show his grief, and you had to respect that was his way.

This was how we all were now. We'd learned to live with each other again. It was a new kind of happiness that had taken us a while to get used to.

At midday the doorbell rang. Mum, who looked so gorgeous in a flowing purple dress, her hair piled up, and some flashing Christmas tree earrings that I teased her about later, gave me a look I recognized. It meant that the Witkins were here. Mum did *not* like Julie Witkin. I'd overheard her arguing with Dad in their bedroom a few weeks ago:

"Why do we have to have *them* here? For *Christmas?*"

"I just thought it would be nice. They were going to spend it at their beach house, but it got termites."

Mum had laughed so loudly that I'd jumped back from the door and switched ears.

"Cece," said Dad, quite seriously, "they've been good to me."

I left after that. And the next thing I knew it was back on with the Witkins coming for Christmas lunch.

"Come in, come in!" Mum sang, in that old way of hers, because when she was well she was still the best at putting on a show and making people feel special in her house.

"Cece, you look *divine*," said Julie Witkin.

"Gosh, well, you look simply *stunning*," Mum replied.

That was how they always spoke to each other. It was pretty funny because I was sure Julie didn't like Mum either.

At that moment, Sophie held out the skirt of her dress, went on her tiptoes, and dropped again.

"And you look adorable too, Soph," said Mum. "Why don't you tell Summer all about what presents you got?"

"You won't believe it, Summer!" said Soph.

Poor Soph. She was who she was. I shuddered to think of how horrible I'd been to her, especially because she was improving. I smiled and patted the floor next to me. Sophie tiptoed over with her arms floating out as if she were auditioning for *Swan Lake*. (Okay, she was improving a tiny bit.)

"Guess what I got," she said.

"Um...An iPod? A scooter? A...cuddly unicorn?"

"A unicorn? I'm eleven! *Wrong*. A guitar." She assumed the air guitar position and pretended to be rocking out, making *nuh-nuh-nuh* noises. "And guess what else?"

"You're...going to give us a concert later?" Sophie was famous for her post-barbecue concerts.

"No, silly. I can't play it yet. It's that Mum says you can teach me!"

"Oh! Right!" I dared not look at Wren or Mum in that moment, or I'd never be able to keep up the bizarre zombie grin I had on my face in place of a genuine smile.

"Thank you, Summer, that would be darling of you," said Julie. "Milo, have you said hello to everyone yet?" She nudged him forward.

Milo did his usual awkward windshield-wiper wave. Then he plonked down next to Wren without saying a word. Only I saw the tiny nudge that meant hello. Wren and Milo were a lot cuter than they thought. They were really private, especially around Dad and Mr. Witkin. I still had no idea if they were a couple or not but I knew it was special, whatever it was.

Sometimes I think that what Wren told me that day on the porch was so huge for her that she had to back off for a while. I hadn't figured out how to make a moment like that happen again, but that didn't mean I'd given up.

"Is it too early for champagne?" said Julie, brandishing a bottle.

"I'd say it's exactly the right time!" said Mum, and she winked at me as she passed on her way to get the champagne glasses.

Half an hour later, the doorbell rang again. All of a sudden I felt self-conscious about my face, as if I'd suddenly remembered I had eyes, eyebrows, a mouth, and that they needed not to betray the way I was feeling inside.

It was Gabe.

Every time we saw him I wondered if this would be the day that he'd remember me and us. Only, as much as I hoped for it, I was scared of it, too.

Gabe's memory of life before and even after the bomb—up until the second time he'd woken up in hospital and we'd been there—was like a shattered glass. There were a few large pieces that he could pick up in his bare hands, hundreds of tiny shards that were too dangerous to go near, and other bits that had been cast so far away that they still hadn't been found.

This had been hard for me to take but even harder to watch.

The holes in his memory weren't exactly empty—they were full of pain. First of all, he had to relearn how sick his mum was. And then he had to confront what it meant that his dad had left him alone in London, at fifteen, and hadn't been seen or heard from since. As if that wasn't enough, he must have sensed, no matter how hard we tried not to let it show, that all of us Jackmans wanted him to remember that last day with Floyd.

He almost had.

One evening, we'd been having dinner in the garden when one by one we'd noticed that Gabe had stopped moving. He was staring into a space that none of us could see. The whole table went still. When Gabe started speaking, I think we all understood where he was taking us. Some of us held onto each other. Mum held onto Gabe.

"First it's black, and then suddenly I'm there in the station. I'm by myself. I don't know where we'd been earlier that day. But we'd said good-bye and I wasn't standing with him when it happened." Gabe swallowed. "Floyd is walking away from me. He's with a girl, actually. But I can't remember how he knew her. I remember her face; she's pretty, with short black hair. I don't know if you knew about her?"

We all shook our heads, but far in the back of my mind I realized I *had* known that, just not in a way that I could have remembered on my own.

"They are way off in the distance. I can just see them underneath the clock, and I call out to him and say, 'Hey, mate, you left me with the wrong guitar!' Floyd turns around and I can tell even from far away that he means for it to be in my hands."

Gabe looked me in the eyes and it reached inside to squeeze my heart. I felt sure he must be remembering us in that moment. But then he said, "Floyd was so kind. Well, you all knew that," and the moment was gone. He was back in the station.

"The next thing I remember is a noise and white light and everything flying. I'm lifted off my feet, thrown backward, and I must have smashed my head against something. I get up quickly—or at least I think I do—and everyone is screaming. I realize I'm screaming too, and I'm still holding his guitar. I'm gripping it so tightly, and staring deep into the sound hole. It's as if it's pulling me inside, somewhere safe." He cupped his hands into a circle. "Sorry, that must sound strange when you know what was going on around me."

"No," I said. "It doesn't."

"I can't . . . I can't talk about everything. I can't say the words for the things I see."

"It's all right, Gabe," said Mum.

"From that point on it's like I'm watching myself do things on CCTV, but it's not me. It's some other kid. I see him putting the guitar down. He looks at it for a long time—or maybe just a second, I have no idea. He picks up his bag. A woman comes toward him and she's shouting at him and she looks frantic but he can't hear a word she's saying. There's smoke everywhere, and small fires, but he sees some daylight that he wants to walk toward. So he just pushes her aside and he goes.

"He walks for ages. His head is pounding. It's as if he's the only one going in that direction. Everyone else is running toward where he's just come from. And no matter how far he walks he can still hear screaming."

Gabe looked at Mum suddenly. "I'm so sorry. Should I stop?"

Mum was crying, but she smiled and stroked Gabe's hair over the long silver scar that his hair wouldn't grow over, where they'd found a blood clot. First they thought it was from being knocked down by a car when he landed back in Melbourne, but later they figured it would have been from the blast. Head injuries don't always tell you they're there. Sometimes damage can be done deep inside and it takes a while to bring you down. Gabe made it to the airport, cleaned himself up over a washbasin at Gatwick, and boarded a plane using the official letter that allowed him to fly on his own. That whole time, he didn't say a word to anyone about what had just happened to him.

The driver of the car they thought had knocked him down just a few blocks from home had sworn that she hadn't hit Gabe hard. The whole time Gabe was in a coma, she was trying to convince the hospital that there was more to his injuries than they knew. She swore that Gabe had stumbled onto the road and hit the ground, that her car hadn't been traveling that fast, that there was no way she could have caused all of Gabe's injuries. In a way, the car accident had saved him because it got him to the right place. If he'd collapsed somewhere else, they might not have gotten to him in time.

So destiny was beautiful and ugly. We had all lost, and we had all found. Gran had said to me once that new seeds have to start out in a dark place. It's the light you give them afterward that makes them grow healthy and strong.

Sometimes my family seemed to have all the answers we needed: that Floyd had died happy, and that he *had* definitely died. I know that much had been obvious to everyone else but there had always been a part of me that had tried to write myself a different story.

When the dust had settled, Mum and I had fought a few times over what I knew about Gabe and why I'd been so sure that we needed to find him. I wouldn't tell her. It wasn't a story for everyone to know. Only me, Bee, Floyd, and one other, for now.

Of course, Gabe had been curious, too.

"What made you come looking for me?" he'd asked, the second time we'd visited him in the hospital. "I hadn't known your brother very long, and I never met you. Or did we meet? Have I just forgotten?"

I felt sure that the whole truth had to be a place Gabe got to in his own time. Truth was clearer and brighter if you found it yourself.

"We didn't meet, but I knew you must have meant a lot to him. He wouldn't give his Ibanez Artwood to just anyone, you know."

"But you didn't know he'd done that, did you?"

"Oh. Not exactly. But he'd written something on some song sheets he left for me: "Gabe. Ibanez Artwood." And I got curious, that's all."

Gabe frowned, as if something I'd said had jogged a memory. "Which songs were they?"

I told him the names of the five songs.

"Can you look in my stuff?" Gabe asked. "I think he gave them to me, too."

I opened the small cupboard by the side of his bed. There they were, folded in half and half again. An exact copy of the ones I'd once had.

"But my name isn't on these," he said.

I wanted to tell him the truth so much, but instead I said, "Maybe we could play them together one day."

Gabe nodded and smiled, then he looked nervous. "I don't know if I can say this."

"You can say anything to me," I told him.

"Well, it's just . . . I know Floyd was your family, not mine, and we hadn't known each other very long, but he still felt like . . ."

My mouth was dry and I could hardly get the words out. "A brother?"

"Yeah. Is that okay for me to say?"

"He was a really good brother. So I get it."

Gabe was back in school now, repeating a year. The Child Protection Service had found him somewhere to live because his mum needed someone with her all the time and, despite Gabe's begging, they wouldn't let it be him. Mum and Dad wanted to become Gabe's legal guardians, but it wasn't that easy. It didn't matter, though. In our heads I think that's how we all saw ourselves, anyway. We were all guardians for one another.

———

Dad walked in with a big grin on his face and his arm around Gabe's shoulder. He had to stretch for that because Gabe was now taller than him.

"Hey, it's our main man Gabe!" said Dad.

Oh Dad, I thought.

"Don't worry, Gabe, that's not your official title," said Wren dryly.

Gabe shrugged and looked at Dad. "I don't mind it." He put his hair behind his ears the way I remembered. It had grown back quickly after his operation.

Wren held up her hand for a high five (ironic, of course, being Wren). Milo did, too, and after him Sophie, so then I felt I had to as well. When our hands touched I hoped he wouldn't see any trace of how, when he was in a room, he was everywhere to me.

"Hey," he said.

"Hey."

He took off the guitar case that was on his back. It was the Ibanez Artwood.

"Jam later?" he said to me.

"Definitely. But no Christmas carols."

"What's that?" said Dad. "No Christmas carols? Nonsense!" And suddenly the room filled with that terrible Slade song and everyone groaned, except for Dad and Sophie. They were dancing.

the other side of
summer

At half past two, Mum caught me looking at the clock. Everyone was lounging in the garden, overstuffed with Dad's feast. Dad had left on his special mission over an hour ago. Gabe was on a beanbag by the lemon tree, practicing some riffs, and Bee was at his feet.

"Not long now," said Mum.

I was standing just inside the sliding doors, to get away from the sun for a bit and also because I couldn't sit still. Mum put both arms around me and rested her face on the top of my head. She could still do that—although I *was* a bit taller, it was nothing to get excited about. But it didn't seem to matter at all. I didn't feel powerless and tiny anymore. Well, hardly ever.

"They're here!"

It was Wren, shouting from the front room, which was now her and Mum's art room and had a view to the street.

"Let me! Let me!" I shouted, my bare feet thundering on the wooden floors, through the living room, and down the hallway.

I took a deep breath as two tall shapes appeared behind the glass panel of our front door. Finally, after two years in which time had both crawled and flown, here was the one person who knew everything. Dad had brought her to me.

When I opened the door Mal and I screamed at each other. We hugged hard and messily and she lifted me right off the ground, and we screamed even more.

"Let the poor girl inside, Summer!" said Dad, laughing.

Everyone had gathered at the door now, but we didn't care what we looked like. We screamed again, still holding on tightly, jumping on the spot.

"Right, folks, I think they might need a few more moments." Mum herded everyone back into the house.

"Oh my goodness, look at you," said Mal.

"What?"

"You have absolutely no tan!"

We laughed so hard we were almost cackling, holding on to each other.

"You are so tall! How can you be this tall?" I screeched. "I grew, too, and now you can't even tell!"

"Are you going to actually let me in, Summer? Because I came a very long way, you know, and I have certain needs, like the need to use a bathroom. Hopefully you have an indoor toilet here because I've heard about dunnies and I'm not using one."

I thought I would never stop smiling as I led her inside. I wanted Mal to talk forever.

"Also, I need to know how long it's going to be before I see a kangaroo."

The adults were asleep in the living room and the mood was mellow. It would be night soon. The hours of the day stretched generously behind us and it was the cicadas' turn to make all the noise. We'd had pavlova *and* Christmas pudding. We were feeling full and happy.

"Shall we have that jam now?" said Gabe.

"I'm up for that," said Mal. "Has Summer told you what an amazing voice I have?"

Gabe looked awkward for a moment, because I had in fact told him that she sounded like she was having her appendix taken out with no anesthetic. And *I* felt awkward because watching Mal and Gabe talk made me feel like my two worlds were colliding.

"She did tell me," he said, but his eyes began to twinkle.

Mal threw her head back and laughed. "I'm joking, don't worry."

"Well, I say we get out of here," said Wren. "Who wants to go to the river?"

"Yes! Me, definitely. The river." Mal nudged me and I refused to look at her.

"At night!" Sophie breathed. "Wait, does this mean you're not taking me?"

Nobody replied. We all looked at one another. During the afternoon, Sophie had fallen completely under Mal's spell and she'd been as quiet and wide-eyed as a loris. Of course she had another side, I told myself. Everybody does.

"You're coming, Soph," I said. "This can be your first guitar lesson."

The moon was huge and flat, more like a space where something had once been. Like a sound hole.

It was still warm and there weren't many people about. Gabe had the Ibanez Artwood on his back, and I had my own guitar on mine. We all talked as we walked along. Sophie screamed when a bat flew over us, but she calmed right down when she saw how impressed Mal was that there were such enormous bats here.

"That's amazing. Huge bats! You guys! What else am I going to see on this walk?"

"Um, possums?" said Milo.

"POSSUMS!" Mal shouted.

Everyone laughed at her, with her, near her, as she pointed out all the things that were new. I loved seeing this place through her eyes.

Then Mal and I hung back for a while, still getting used to being in each other's space again and wanting to relish small moments of it in peace.

"So what's new back home?" I said. "Has anything changed?"

"I don't know, really. It all seems the same to me. I guess you don't notice change so much when it happens right under your nose."

I slowed down some more.

"But . . . am I the same?" I asked. "Because you are. I think."

"You're the same and different. You're my best friend, Summer. That will never change."

———

Gabe said he knew a place that was perfect.

We walked across a deserted cricket field and

through a densely wooded area. Now we were on a rough pathway I'd never been down before. Gabe and I were a little way ahead of the others.

"I didn't know you spent much time around here," I said, trying to hide my curiosity as much as I could while still searching for the answers I wanted.

"I come here a lot. It's weird. Before, I used to come with my mates, sit under the bridge in the same spot. It was just a hiding place for us, I suppose. But now . . . I don't know, this will sound crazy."

"It won't, I promise."

He smiled at me. "Okay. When I go to the bridge these days, it's like I'm looking for something."

"Or someone?" I couldn't stop the words from coming out.

He caught my eye. We didn't speak. And then he stopped suddenly and looked ahead. "This is it. We have to climb over this fence and then down. It's a bit steep. Maybe this was a dumb idea. Will you be all right with your guitar?"

"I'll be fine." I looked back to make sure the others were far enough away that they wouldn't hear me. "Gabe, when you stopped just then, did you remember something?"

He squeezed his eyes shut and opened them again quickly. "It's not there. I mean, it's there but I can't reach it, Summer. It's like . . . You know when someone loses an arm or a leg and they say they can feel it even though they can't see it? Like that."

At that moment I felt Bee slide alongside me, positioning herself so that my hand was on her back. Us three, again.

I felt more certain than ever that it was only a matter of time.

———

"A waterfall? You guys live near a waterfall!"

Mal was still being hilarious. I could tell that everyone loved her.

"You live near the National Gallery," said Milo.

"Oh, do I? I've never been," Mal replied, laughing, pretending to look guilty.

It was actually a very small waterfall, but it was wide and loud, kicking up a long thick line of frothy cream at the bottom that carried on, tripping over rocks and disappearing around a bend. The best thing was the set of three flat rocks Gabe had brought us down to, like a tiered stage. It was perfect. That, and the powerful noise of the water, so I could sing and be loud without feeling shy.

Mal, Sophie, and Milo sat on the lowest rock. Sophie had her guitar in her lap and was softly strumming the two easy chords I'd shown her, with her chin resting on the top and her bottom lip pouting in concentration. Wren and I sat on the third, highest rock, with our feet on the second, and Gabe stood behind us. I looked around at him as he fine-tuned his strings.

" 'The Other Side'?" I said to him.

He nodded, serious but not solemn. It was Floyd's song, and we'd finished it for him.

"Wren?" I said. "Ready?"

She smiled.

I wanted to cry, but I wasn't filled with sadness. I was okay.

We were okay.

THE OTHER SIDE

By Floyd Jackman, Summer Jackman, and Gabe de Souza

Capo on first fret

CHORDS:

A A/C# D Dmaj9 Dsus2 D6(add9) D6(add9)/B
D6(add9)/F# E E6 E7

INTRO:

A Dmaj9 A Dmaj9

VERSE ONE:

```
A                 Dmaj9
She comes to me in whispers
```

```
  A           Dmaj9
In music on the page
```

```
      E             Dsus2 Dmaj9 D6(add9)
The notes I carry with me
```

```
       E              Dsus2 Dmaj9 D6(add9)
She plays them like I played them.


A            Dmaj9
My other side is secret


     A          Dmaj9
The secret has a name


    E            Dsus2  Dmaj9  D6(add9)
I traveled far to reach you


E            Dsus2 Dmaj9 D6(add9)
To where a face will find a name.
```

PRE-CHORUS:
```
                  F#m
I'm out of time and place


               D
But when I see your face


                  E E6 E7
I know you know where I am.
```

CHORUS:
```
A       D6(add9)/B
Closer to you


        A/C#          D
I'm getting closer to you
```

```
         A                    D6(add9)/B
And it's a song that pulls me through

          A/C#      D
Bringing me closer to you

          A
Closer to you.

VERSE TWO:

               Dmaj9
He comes to me in starlight,

       A         D maj9
And near but far away

    E              Dsus2  Dmaj9  D6(add9)
I close my eyes and count now

       E              Dsus2  Dmaj9  D6(add9)
He's shining in the distance.

A               Dmaj9
The other side is secret

        A              Dmaj9
On the other side of the world

       E              Dsus2  Dmaj9  D6(add9)
The other side of reason

       E              Dsus2  Dmaj9  D6(add9)/F#
The other side of a girl.
```

CHORUS

SOLO:

A Dmaj9 A Dmaj9 A

VERSE THREE:

       Dmaj9
It comes to me in heartache

  A   Dmaj9
For things we left behind,

    E   Dsus2 Dmaj9 D6(add9)
You cannot take them with you,

    E   Dsus2 Dmaj9
The pieces are reminders

     A   A/C# Dmaj9
That come to me in whispers

     A   Dmaj9
You're music on the page

    E   Dsus2 Dmaj9 D6(add9)
In notes I carry with me

    E   Dsus2 Dmaj9 D6(add9) D6(add9)/F#
I play them like you played them.

CHORUS

OUTRO:

        A   D6(add9)/B
Closer to you

        A/C#   D
Closer to you

        A   D6(add9)/B
Closer to you

        A/C#   D
Closer to you

ACKNOWLEDGMENTS

Charlie, I can honestly say that this story would not have been the same without you. No matter what I've said in the past—usually when you've rolled in something disgusting—you, Charlie, are a very good dog.

Aaron, Madeleine, and Jonah, thank you for all of our river adventures and for being mine. You three amaze me.

Zoe Walton, my publisher, thank you so much for believing in this story. Bronwyn O'Reilly, my editor, your attention to detail is both terrifying and brilliant. Thank you both for being so encouraging, wise, and patient. Thank you also to Vanessa Lanaway and to Victoria Stone for proofreading.

Thank you, Penguin Random House Australia, for the first opportunity to share this story. And thank you to Emilia Rhodes and everyone at HarperCollins US for giving it a new place to land, and new readers to find.

Astred Hicks—thank you for another beautiful jacket.

Tim Reid, I remember the exact moment I said "Wouldn't it be cool if . . ." and I'm so thankful that you said yes.

Caroline Green and Fiona Wood, I don't know if you will believe me when I tell you how important you both were to this book, but please try.

Thank you Louise Burns for your notes on an early draft. And thanks Rebecca Ryan for telling me about emergence delirium one day on a bench in school when we were supposed to be watching netball practice.

Nina Kenwood and Bronte Coates, I love our writing group so much. Thank you for the support you've given me.

Thank you to Justine Larbalestier, whose novel *Magic or Madness* inspired me to pick up this story again after I'd neglected it for too long. Thanks also to all the #LoveOzYA authors whose work has nourished me since I came to live in Australia.

Thank you to the Wurundjeri Elders for permission

to use a fictional name for part of the Yarra River, and to Charley Woolmore and Daniel Ducrou for helping with this matter.

I've been creative with the geography of this part of Melbourne to suit the story I wanted to tell, but I couldn't have told it without the real stretch of Yarra that I walk by every day. It's a beautiful place that always restores me, so I'd like to respectfully acknowledge the traditional land of the Kulin nation.

Finally, thank you to my fantastic parents, Susan and Christopher.

31901060641992